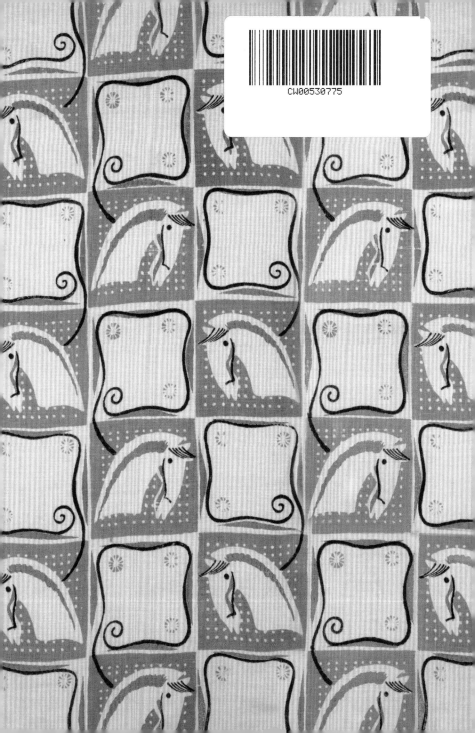

PRINCES IN THE LAND

Persephone Book Nº63
Published by Persephone Books Ltd 2006

First published 1938 by Victor Gollancz Ltd

© 1938 The Estate of Joanna Cannan

Endpapers taken from 'Horse's Head', a 1938–9
screen-printed linen by Lucienne Day
© V&A Images/Victoria and Albert Museum

Typeset in ITC Baskerville by Keystroke,
Jacaranda Lodge, Wolverhampton

Colour by Banbury Litho

Printed and bound by Biddles Ltd, King's Lynn

ISBN 1903155533

Persephone Books Ltd
59 Lamb's Conduit Street
London WC1N 3NB
020 7242 9292

www.persephonebooks.co.uk

PRINCES IN THE LAND

by

JOANNA CANNAN

✳ ✳ ✳

PERSEPHONE BOOKS
LONDON

'Instead of your fathers you shall have children, whom you shall make princes in the land.'

Psalm 45, verse 16

CONTENTS

✱ ✱ ✱

PRINCES IN THE LAND

CHAPTER ONE

✷ ✷ ✷

The Bad Traveller

'Mother – quick! The basin!'

'Oh, Patricia, not again! It's really too disgusting.'

'Oh, Mother, Pat can't help being sick,' said loyal Angela.

'I know she can't,' said Blanche Crispin, making a face as she stooped and pulled an enamel basin from under the seat of the second class compartment. 'But I'm not accustomed to this kind of thing. It was really too bad of your father.'

'Father couldn't help the nasty Boers killing him,' said Angela.

Blanche said, 'It was quite unnecessary for him to volunteer. Sometimes I think he only did it to annoy me.' She did not usually speak with so much lack of reserve before her small daughters, but she was tired to death, much too hot in her blue serge travelling dress and disgusted by the menial offices she was performing for Patricia.

'Poor Father,' said Angela.

Relegated to the nurseries, shrubberies and backstairs of a succession of furnished houses, neither of Almeric Crispin's daughters had seen much of him, but they had liked him. He

1

had seldom been at home, but, when he had, it had been his custom to pay delightful impromptu visits to their nurseries, where he had petted Angela, called Patricia a young devil, put Nurse into a good temper and left before he got bored or came to the end of his amusing anecdotes. When he had come to say goodbye to them in his Yeomanry uniform with an armful of monkeys-on-sticks, tin tops and dying pigs from the Strand pavements, they had adored him; and now that he was dead for Queen and Country, they worshipped him, and each cherished above all things a staring photograph of a heavy-featured man with a drooping moustache, mounted on a showy black charger. They were women before they realised that Almeric Crispin had been annoyed that they had been born at all, disappointed because they were not boys, and constantly exasperated by the tiresome expense they caused him.

Patricia, having been sick and, as Blanche reproachfully pointed out, brought up nothing, leaned her carroty head against the padded partition and enquired in a faint voice, 'How much longer?'

Blanche consulted her watch. It was of ruby-red enamel, ornamented with a flying dove in pearls, and was pinned by a brooch, representing a ribbon bow, to her unimpressive bosom.

'Two hours more.'

Patricia sighed. 'Oh dear, I do feel so ill.'

Angela, producing chalks and a pinkish paper volume from the series *Books for the Bairns*, suggested, 'Do some chalking.'

'Oh dear, I can't,' moaned Patricia, 'I shall die before we get to Hulver, I know I shall.'

'Don't be silly, Patricia,' said Blanche sharply. 'Nibble a biscuit and don't vex Mother.'

Patricia burst into tears.

Angela was frightened. Patricia, though a year younger, was far the more vigorous, ran faster, jumped higher and seldom cried. 'Oh, Mother,' said Angela, 'can't we stop the train or something? I'm sure she'll die.'

'Don't be silly and hysterical,' said Blanche. 'Patricia's quite well except for this stupid train sickness. She only says things like that because she's sorry for herself. You should forget yourself, Patricia, and think how disagreeable it is for me.'

Patricia stopped crying and felt shamed. Poor little Edwardian, she knew how, in the bright cold downstairs world where ladies and gentlemen lived, it was disgusting to be sick, improper to want to go to the lavatory, rude to hiccup and absolutely impossible, however bad your cold was or whatever came up in your throat, to spit. Nurse had bullied her, and boxed her ears and told her that she was ugly, but she wished that Nurse was here now and Mother travelling first class as she used to do. 'Shall we have a nurse when we get to Hulver?' she asked hopefully.

Blanche said, 'I don't know. We are entirely dependent on your grandfather and I have no idea what arrangements will be made.' She shut her lips tightly. She was both virtuous and proud, had been rich before Almeric had squandered her fortune, and, in more ways than one, it hurt her to think that she was now dependent on bad old Lord Waveney.

Though Angela herself was perfectly at home among ladies and gentlemen, had sweet manners, never made a mess

* * *

on the tablecloth and could travel all day in a non-corridor carriage without physical inconvenience, she understood why Patricia wanted to have a nurse again: that sort of person didn't mind if you were sick. Why? Angela understood that, too. It was because they were different. Just as cows are there to give milk, and hens to lay eggs, and dogs to retrieve game, they were there to come and clear up the mess when you rang the bell. She could see that all this was hard on Mother, who had been brought up to ring bells and had now no bells to ring; but she could also see that it was hard on Patricia – it must be awful to be train-sick and twice as awful to be train-sick in front of Mother. Sorry for both of them – a divine state, perhaps, but quite natural to little empty-headed Angela – she said, 'Perhaps we shall be changing again soon, Patricia.'

Their journey was very nearly the classic one from Barmouth to Yarmouth: it was, in fact, from Criccieth to Norwich, and they had already changed at Shrewsbury, Birmingham and Stafford. A narrow margin of time worried Blanche to distraction; a long wait drove her crazy with impatience, but once out of the swaying train, Patricia revived: at Birmingham she had even eaten a Bath bun and said that she felt better.

'No,' said Blanche. 'Thank goodness we don't change again. We get out at Norwich and your grandfather will have sent a carriage.'

'Can I sit on the box?' asked Patricia.

'Certainly not. It wouldn't be safe if you feel as faint as you make out, lolling about there. Do sit up, dear. Your nice pelisse is all crumpled. I don't know what your grandfather will think of you.'

Patricia sat up and Angela went to sit beside her. She read aloud the story of Snow White and Rose Red, and then she looked out of the window and described the country through which they were passing – Patricia couldn't look out herself because the racing telegraph posts made her giddy. Blanche in her corner brooded over days gone by . . . if only she'd had the strength of mind that day on the grouse moor to refuse the Honourable Almeric, surely in spite of her teeth there'd have been other chances; she'd had a fine head of hair and excellent manners; she hadn't been fast, like some girls, or slow, like others; she'd always dressed smartly but unobtrusively, in fact, like a lady Yet fast girls and slow girls had got off before her – men were such fools – and at twenty-eight, with teeth like hers, it had seemed madness to refuse an offer. And though she had never stayed at Hulver, because it wasn't the kind of house where your mamma would allow you to stay even if by any unlikely chance you got an invitation, she had heard of it, and how could she have foreseen that, only a couple of years after her marriage, Lord Waveney would order his only surviving son to get the hell out of it? If only Angela had been a boy . . . but it wasn't dear little Angela's fault and she was so lovely and so *complaisant* that, if, when the time came, Lord Waveney could be persuaded to do his duty by her and provide for a London season, she was certain to make a magnificent marriage. It was Patricia who ought to have been the boy, thought Blanche irritably; then her carroty hair and hoydenish ways wouldn't have mattered;

even her good points – her physical courage, ability to run, jump and climb, her brilliant horsemanship – would have been better suited to a boy. And what a difference it would have made now! thought Blanche; I should be going back to Hulver as the heir's mother instead of a poor relation; and she looked across at Patricia and said, 'You do look a scarecrow. Why can't you keep tidy like Angela?'

Patricia was dumb, but Angela said, 'It's not her fault. It's my shape that keeps me tidy.'

'Nonsense,' said Blanche. 'It's because you keep still and hold yourself like a lady. Patricia *throws* herself about. When I was a child, I always looked nice. I don't know how I came to have such a daughter.'

'Perhaps it was a mistake,' suggested Patricia. 'Perhaps I was someone's else's. I don't see how you know a baby's yours when you find it under the gooseberry bushes. And supposing your garden hasn't *got* any gooseberry bushes.'

A faint colour came into Blanche's yellow cheeks. She said, 'Don't be a horrid inquisitive little girl, Patricia.'

Presently Angela asked the time and Blanche looked at her watch and said they should get the things out of the rack, so the wicker luncheon basket, the rugs and the umbrellas, Blanche's fitted dressing-case and a hat box were lifted down and piled on the seat, and Blanche smoothed her collar and cuffs, pulled on her gloves, drew down her veil and made Patricia wash her face with a damp sponge from her dressing-case. The sight and the smell of the black-and-white check sponge bag and the feel of a damp sponge on her skin were associated so vividly in Patricia's mind with railway journeys and train-sickness that she was sick again and had barely finished when the train drew into Norwich station. Blanche, however, bundled her out of the carriage, telling her to take Angela's hand and walk properly in case her grandfather was on the platform.

With blackness before her eyes and a rushing sound in her ears, the fainting child forced her wilting legs to follow where Angela guided. She did not then know her grandfather.

When the rushing sound ceased and the blackness cleared away, she found herself sitting in a carriage. The carriage was rolling smoothly through streets; gas lamps were shining in the blue September darkness, and, this being market day, the pavements were crowded. Angela said, 'What a big town! It must be as big as London.'

Blanche replied, 'Don't be silly. Norwich is only a provincial town.'

'What's a provincial town?' asked Angela.

'Any town that isn't London,' said Blanche sweepingly. 'Nobody lives in provincial towns except people like doctors and solicitors, but a great many nice people live in London.'

'Aren't doctors nice?' asked Patricia, who had no feeling for social hairlines and often embarrassed Blanche, who considered herself no snob, by persisting in such crude questions.

Blanche began to say that doctors are very wise men and we should all look up to them, but Angela, finding Patricia revived, had distracted her interest by whispering that there were two lovely grey horses, and Blanche was for once obliged to correct her favourite: it was rude to whisper while grown-up people were speaking. The two girls retreated into the state of snubbed silence which Blanche called being good, and the carriage rolled out of the town into the dark country.

Patricia has forgotten all the details of that journey; she only remembers that she was sick and her mother wasn't very kind about it; but she remembers very clearly arriving at Hulver, stumbling up the steps of Italian marble and finding the big doors open and her grandfather standing in the blaze of light from the four great sparkling chandeliers. He had his wolfhound beside him, and in a very loud voice he told the girls that its name was Shaun, and he made it shake hands with them and was delighted to find that neither of them was frightened. Then he asked if they had had a comfortable journey and Blanche said yes, except that Patricia was such a bad traveller, and, to Patricia's intense surprise, the tall white-haired hawk-nosed man of the world said that he was a bad traveller too; he'd lay a hundred to one, he said, that he was a worse traveller than Patricia; he'd nearly died of sea-sickness, he said, as a youngster going to the Crimea. 'But one grows out of it,' he said to Patricia. 'One grows out of everything,' and his voice changed as he said that, and he looked at Blanche and grinned as though there were a joke between them; but Blanche only turned away.

The girls had biscuits and milk in the house-keeper's room, and they they bathed in a very large and shabby bathroom and went to bed in a very large and shabby bedroom, where their father – so the housekeeper told them – had slept with his two elder brothers when he was a little boy. Blanche

✱ ✱ ✱

dined with Lord Waveney and they kept off the subjects of Almeric, debts, days gone by and the Boer War, and talked about the Radicals, which was the only subject Lord Waveney could think of on which they were likely to agree. After dinner, Blanche withdrew to the yellow drawing-room and the old man, with his wolfhound stretched out beside him, sat over his port, wondering on how many nights in the week you could talk about Radicals, wondering if there was any Crispin at all in those two overdressed children, or if, in spite of his turning Hulver upside down for them, they would grow up to be like Blanche, virtuous women, who would walk in faith and keep the Commandments and burn in hell (he hoped) for their sins of omission. He wasn't quite clear yet which child was Angela and which was Patricia, and he thought that the pretty fair-haired one looked a fool, but he liked the look of the ugly red-headed one – the bad traveller.

CHAPTER TWO

✱ ✱ ✱

Hulver

Ten years, ten months and six days later, Hugh Lindsay, who, as Blanche once pointed out, was nobody, making his way across the hall to the office where he'd been told that he'd find Lord Waveney, bolstered up his fainting courage by asking himself what, after all, there was to these Crispins. They owned this immense house and more land than you could see from its Norman watch-towers, but since the first Baron Waveney had received his disproportionate reward for blows struck at the little battle of Senlac, what had the Crispins done, who had heard of them? Hugh was a Scotsman, had been born and bred in a pink sandstone villa on the outskirts of Peebles. His father was a builder, his mother a daughter of the Manse. He had got himself a scholarship to Glenalmond and another to Oxford and at the time when he went to Hulver he was twenty-eight and a Reader in Literature at Glasgow University. He was never a vain man, but he was proud of what he had done for himself; he had 'got on' for over eight hundred years: busy, purposeful, out for the prizes (though he learned better later), he was battling with the tides of Life, on which they idly, amiably drifted – so he argued and opened the library door, stammered out, 'Can I speak to you, sir?' and stood tongue-tied, spellbound, before what there was to the Crispins. . . .

Yet, ineffective though his arguments were, he was not far wrong in his summing up of the Crispins. Charming, unambitious people, not lacking in talents but devoid of any desire to exploit their talents, they had succeeded one another at Hulver, enjoyed the fruits of Hulver, broken their necks over their own blind ditches when hounds ran towards the Hulver marshlands, and, in one of their yellow hay wagons, drawn by their Suffolk Punches, had jolted across the park to lie among their forebears and tenants, awaiting the pleasure of the benevolent God who had made them Crispins and given them Hulver. They had died self-satisfied, with only a little gentlemanly over-indulgence in wine and a few decorously conducted acts of fornication between them and heaven; they had never tricked, lied, pushed, prevaricated or bartered, and they had never read of 'a fugitive and cloistered virtue, unexercised and unbreathed, that never sallies out and sees her adversary, but slinks out of the race where that immortal garland is to be run for, not without dust and heat.'

Augustus Roderick, twelfth Baron Waveney, was no exception. He was a sound classic, a brilliant soldier, but, having served the State and set a good example to the lower classes by spilling a pint or two of blood on the Crimean snows, he had been content, and glad to retire for the rest of his life to East Anglia, to hunt hounds, shoot pheasants, breed horses and get sons to succeed him at Hulver. He wasn't a good man. He wasn't sober, pious or chaste; but he was honest, charitable,

***

unselfish, long-suffering and brave. His elder sons had been like him. They were handsome laughing boys with only one idea in life – to get home to Hulver; but George had been killed out hunting and Roderick had died of pneumonia in London and then there had only been Almeric, who had been brave enough, handsome enough, but by some freak of heredity quite without grace: where George and Roderick and Lord Waveney himself had sinned like gentlemen, he had misbehaved, as his father at last pointed out, like a counterjumper. Though none of the Crispins had the faintest idea what a counterjumper was, the word had long been the final epithet in the twelfth Baron's queer and coarse vocabulary, and Almeric had taken himself off to live comfortably enough while his wife's money lasted, then seedily, shabbily, as it became more and more necessary to supplement his own absurd income of five hundred a year, in card rooms and on race courses. He hadn't gone to the South African War in any patriotic spirit: he had seen in it a way of escape from his creditors, his long-toothed wife, an accusation of cheating at cards and the importunities of a certain Miss Daisy Dimple; but there is this to be said of him: he died magnificently. The news – the first word of him in nine years that wasn't scandal – had come to Hulver, and Lord Waveney had received it outwardly unmoved but inwardly sorry, sorry, sorry that he had called his last surviving son a bastard and a counterjumper and told him to get the hell out of Hulver. He had done what he could. He had caused a memorial tablet, bearing the text that begins *Greater love hath no man than this* to be placed in the church; he had persuaded the widowed Mrs Featherstone that he was getting to be an old

***

man and that she would find a prettier cottage and a gayer life elsewhere; he had had the nurseries and the drawing-rooms spring-cleaned; he had bought two pure bred Welsh Mountain ponies and invited his daughter-in-law and her two little girls to live with him. Blanche's papa and mamma were dead. A fruitful spouse, a pious prejudice against contraception, and a political career had placed her brother, Edward, in a position of financial embarrassment. After all the bitterness, the spite and the censure, after all the talk of my people and your people, there had been no one to turn to but the bad old man at Hulver. So Blanche had packed up and left with tears the last and smallest of the furnished houses, and she arrived at Hulver in a thoroughly contrary mood, loathing yet determined to insist upon her dependent position.

Lord Waveney had always disliked his daughter-in-law. He wasn't hard to please, could tolerate ignorance, stupidity and most vices, but he couldn't stand foolishness, and Blanche, though she was well-educated, could speak three languages, play the piano, sketch prettily and discuss politics, was quite without wisdom. He wasn't a spiritual man, but he was aware that there were stars above him as well as earth beneath his feet: Blanche lived between the four walls of seeing and hearing; the things that mattered to her, the things she thought about, the things that delighted or troubled her, were clothes, money, manners and social functions. And still she wasn't a cheerful worldling. Life generally bored her, frequently disgusted her; she suffered the boredom, covered up the ordure, and nearly drove Lord Waveney mad with her resigned face and senseless refinements. Tolerance was his

watchword and his dislike wasn't founded on any judgement of
her. He could have forgiven her her worm's-eye view, her
social ruthlessness, her sickening smug materialism, but her
euphemisms, her not-mentioning, made him squirm; he was
exasperated beyond measure by the false humility with which
she took his money. She wasn't an honest snob: she couldn't
say 'labourer' or 'gentleman': she said 'people of our class'
and 'nobody'. And she wasn't an honest gold-digger: she
couldn't say thank-you and keep her soul: she gave in to him
in all things, agreed with him, pandered to him, shutting her
thin lips on the most trivial difference of opinion in the
way that says, 'I can't answer back; I'm a poor relation.' It is
doubtful if, in spite of his good resolutions, he would have
kept her at Hulver but for the sudden, and to Blanche's mind
inexplicable, fancy which he took for Patricia.

In spirit as well as in body Blanche Crispin's two little
daughters were utterly unlike one another. Angela was fair,
blue-eyed and graceful, a little beauty: Patricia was red-haired,
plain, freckled and coltish. Angela was polite, considered
others. 'Yes, Grandad,' and 'No, Grandad,' she lisped, and she
ate nicely, crept past his library door, kept clean, kept cool,
embroidered cushion covers and had a pretty touch on the
piano. Patricia was far from considerate; she charged up and
downstairs like an elephant, leaving footmarks redolent of the
stable on the Italian marble; she upset plates into her lap,
answered him back, rode forbidden ponies and buried her
fancy work under the laurels in the shrubbery. He was, Blanche
would have thought, the last man to love a hoyden; she didn't
understand that the virtues he thought loveliest were courage

and kindness, and, though Angela was kind, she was timid, while Patricia, besides being kind, was recklessly brave. Angela wasn't too timid to ride her well-broken little grey pony; she had a beautiful seat and would take him out hunting, follow a little and return with the groom behind her at the time she had been told; but Patricia shrieked and stormed to ride half-broken horses, gave James the slip, jumped the blind ditches where the family necks had been broken and came home in the dark, dog-tired, walking unsteadily beside a far less exhausted pony. Blanche would not stand for disobedience; she used to pack Patricia off to bed and later in the evening Lord Waveney, having seen her safely settled in the yellow drawing-room, would sneak upstairs with a plate of ginger wafers in one hand and a dish of grapes in the other and his wolfhound padding behind him, to sit on his granddaughter's bed while she recounted her adventures, making maps of the country with grape skins and wafers on the scarlet silk eiderdown, which clashed so horribly with her carroty hair. Blanche never heard of these midnight feasts, for Angela was loyal, the servants worshipped Patricia, and Miss Menzies, the strict Scottish governess, was consumed by a secret passion for Lord Waveney; but she knew, everybody knew, that, while his feeling for Angela was never more than an amused affection, all his hopes, all his ambitions and interests were now for Patricia.

Blanche wouldn't send her daughters to school. Even the best schools were mixed. You didn't know whom your girls would meet, what they'd hear. Schoolgirls wore hideous clothes, grew silly, thought of nothing but games and, instead of learning to talk on subjects that would interest men, giggled together over mysterious unrepeatable jokes of their own. Lord Waveney thought that Angela was silly already; he thought that it would have done both girls good to learn that there were people in the world who didn't live at Hulver with a grandfather whose income was fifteen thousand a year; he thought that that would probably save them a lot of heart-ache later on; but he couldn't bear the thought of parting from Patricia, so he kept his mouth shut and the passionate Miss Menzies continued to educate the Misses Crispin in a manner excellently suited to a way of life which no longer existed. They learned to speak French and German and to read Italian; they learned to play the piano and paint flowers and windmills. They learned to embroider in silk on satin, while their maid darned their stockings, tucked their fine longcloth nightgowns and ran up their cotton dresses.

When Patricia looks back on her childhood, she sees it as a bright fantastic landscape, lovely but incredible, a landscape before which you'd stand and never say, 'Where is it? Let's go there', for it's Arcady, and obviously you can't go there. Hulver is still standing; at the foot of the park the river meanders through its king-cup meadows; the oak trees grow green and russet and stand bare in the woods that shelter the sly old Hulver foxes; flat as a pancake the salty marshlands stretch to the sea. But it isn't the same Hulver, for the old man is gone and the stiff great lady and the two little girls and the wolfhound and all the horses from the stable; and we don't live that kind of life now: it was useless; it was idle. Now we all start equal – get back there! – your toe's over the line – but still, though Hugh can't see it, we won't finish equal: God's favourite will win.

Patricia doesn't know much about pictures. For eleven years she ate rice pudding and stewed rhubarb under a Rubens and it's not that which turns out connoisseurs of art. But she thinks that looking back on her childhood is like looking at a Turner: there's the same glow on it, the same 'light that never was on sea or land'; and it's cracking: soon there won't be any Turners and there won't be any childhood like hers. Perhaps that's as well, for it's no joke leaving Arcady, and it's a few now who can remain there. Angela has, and, consequently, to Patricia there's always a remoteness about her; she's the figure for ever static in the foreground of the picture, unreal as the chasmed mountains, the lake like a mirror, the promontory castle and strange, too graceful trees. Angela knows it and she is sorry and she writes and asks Patricia to stay at the Villa des Hirondelles, and now that Patricia is less tied she could go, but she doesn't: you can't step back into Arcady once you're out of the frame. . . .

Angela's birthday – unlike Patricia's which is in January – falls conveniently and charmingly on May Day, and the year that she was eighteen Lord Waveney did what Blanche had been hinting at for eight years: he took a furnished house in Grosvenor Square for the season, installed Blanche and Angela with an appropriate staff and hurried back to Hulver. Angela took to society as a duck to water. Exquisite in white satin and pearls, she danced her way into the hearts of three of the most eligible young men in London; during the tea interval at the Eton and Harrow match she refused Mr Hollins because he was in beer; at Cowes, she refused Lord Cremer because he wasn't a nice man, and at Goodwood she accepted Victor Langdale, who had ten thousand a year of his own and three nice places coming to him. Blanche was delighted; Langdale's people were delighted; Lord Waveney said in rather a queer voice that it was extremely suitable and Patricia was thrilled till she met Victor, a pink young man with china-blue eyes and hair as golden as Angela's, who could and did express all life was to him and all his reactions to it in the two simple sentences, 'Hellish, eh?' and 'Ripping, what?'

Blanche considered long engagements tiresome and, as Angela and Victor had nothing to wait for, they were married in the autumn at St George's, Hanover Square. Patricia was a bridesmaid in spite of much opposition from Blanche, who had set her heart on crimson velvet dresses, which would, of course, clash too frightfully with Patricia's unfortunate hair. 'But I must have Pat,' said Angela and substituted a more effective reason than the sentimental one that she knew Blanche would consider mawkish. 'It would look funny if we didn't.' 'Peculiar, eh?' said Victor, heroically producing a third adjective, and Angela gave him a dazzling smile and said, 'We could have sapphire blue instead of crimson – you'd like that, wouldn't you, Victor?' 'Ripping, what?' said Victor, so Patricia in sapphire blue was chief bridesmaid, and more than one elderly gentleman told Blanche that she looked like a picture by Burne Jones or that other fellow, and young Lord Windermere, who was Victor's best man, told Angela that her sister looked a jolly kid; and Angela, though she was being married and had been darkly informed by Blanche that morning that marriage had an unpleasant side to it, was composed enough to remember his remark, so that as soon as Patricia was 'out' she invited her to stay at Copthorne, the house in Leicestershire which Victor had taken till Clove Park, Upholt Hall and Finlay Castle came to him; and she also invited Lord Windermere.

Patricia's coming-out had been a sorry affair compared to Angela's. Patricia at eighteen was angular, freckled and troubled by pimples on her shoulders. Though she was boisterous at home, she was mouse-like at parties; what she had to say could only be said to understanding people like her grandfather, and in company the only subject on which she would open her mouth was horses. Blanche said quite openly that she didn't want to drag a silent spotty daughter about London, and Patricia went out to the stable and wept on the necks of the horses, but not because she wanted a London season: she much preferred to remain at Hulver and only wept because Blanche, whom she wanted so much to love, so often wounded her.

Lord Waveney, hurt himself, pursued Patricia to the stable and found her weeping. He sat down on a cornbin and said, 'Your mother often says things she doesn't mean. Of course you shall have your London season.'

Patricia explained that she didn't want it. She sobbed into Black August's mane, 'I don't want to go to London. I hate young men and tight clothes. I know I've got spots and I can't speak and my hair comes down. I want to stay at home with you and Young Shaun and the horses.' 'All right, all right, you shall,' said Lord Waveney, and he nibbled oats and said, 'I'll tell you what, Pat – we'll have a coming-out ball for you here, at Hulver.' So the ballroom was opened and spring-cleaned and half filled with speechless young men and shiny-faced girls from the neighbourhood and an insolent London band played tunes that nobody knew and Angela brought a large smart bored party. Patricia's hair came down and Blanche entered the library just as Lord Windermere was doing it up for her, and pretended quite successfully that she had seen nothing, but made up her mind that Patricia should marry Lord Windermere. When Angela's invitation came, she said, 'You'd better go. That Windermere boy is sure to be there and he showed every sign of being attracted.'

Patricia, blushing crimson, said, 'He didn't, and anyhow I don't want him to.'

'Don't be silly,' said Blanche. 'You've no looks, you know. You can't expect to pick and choose like dear Angela.'

'I don't want to,' said Patricia. 'I don't want to marry any-one.' This wasn't strictly true: sometime, somewhere, she'd meet the one man there was for every woman, but you couldn't tell Blanche that – you couldn't tell her anything except how many buttons you intended to have on your new dress or what the Rector's wife had said about Lady X.

Patricia went off to Copthorne and blushed when she shook hands with Lord Windermere. Angela sent them out hunting and one evening, as they jogged back through the wet spring twilight from the last hunt of the season Windermere stammered out his proposal. 'Oh, Jimmy,' said Patricia, 'I do like you, but not like that, and anyhow I don't want to marry anyone.'

* * *

'If you like me, you might get to care more,' suggested
Lord Windermere, and, looking between his horse's ears, he
said that he thought a lot of nonsense was talked about this
love business: the important thing, he thought, was to be
friends and then you could have a jolly time together. Patricia
was shocked. In spite of having Blanche for a mother, she
expected to find in love the answer to rose and nightingale;
the pity she'd felt for this unexacting young man changed
abruptly to scorn and she told him sharply that the world
was full of girls whom he could have a jolly time with. They
rode home in silence and next morning, in accordance with
contemporary good manners, he left Copthorne. Angela
said, 'What a pity,' and Victor said, 'Hellish, eh?' and Patricia
went for long walks alone and lost the Dandie Dinmonts while
she wondered whether, after all, she was a romantic idiot,
or whether she'd been right and walking the earth at this
moment, waiting for her, wondering sometimes too if she
really existed, was the one man meant for her. . . .

She met him two years later, as she travelled home from
another visit to Copthorne. The train was moving out of
Leicester Station and the guard yelled a protest as a porter
pushed him and his Gladstone bag unceremoniously into her
compartment. He fell over her feet and begged her pardon
and then he said, 'Oh lord, this is a first class carriage.' Patricia,
forgetting how often Blanche had told her not to speak to
strange men, said, 'Well, you can't get out now,' and he agreed,
and yanked his bag into the rack beside her dressing-case.

Patricia opened the *Tatler*. Hugh whistled through his
teeth for a bit and then he jumped up, said, 'Excuse me,' and

✳ ✳ ✳

began to pull down his bag again. It was a very old bag and the straps at the sides weren't done up, and, as he heaved it out of the rack, it opened and spewed forth a stream of books, shoes, underclothing, a wooden-backed hair-brush, a damp sponge, a tooth-brush and a safety razor. Hugh said, 'Oh my God!' and Patricia burst out laughing.

The sponge had fallen into her lap, the books round her head, and the razor bounced off the seat and rolled under it. 'Oh, I say, I'm sorry,' said Hugh and he stood there passing his fingers distractedly through his brown hair and she saw how young and thin and shabby he was, and thought how cruelly fate had treated him by pushing him into a first class carriage with an unknown female and scattering round her head his pathetic possessions. Jumping up and straightening her hat, which *The Poetical Works of George Herbert* had knocked sideways, Patricia said, 'Something's rolled under the seat. Let's fish for it with my umbrella.'

Hugh went on his hands and knees and scraped under pipes with Patricia's five guinea gold-mounted umbrella. Patricia collected the books. She loved poetry, doted indiscriminately on Tennyson, Browning, Newbolt, Kipling and Whyte-Melville, and she asked what George Herbert was like and Hugh snatched the book from her and, still kneeling on the floor, read aloud 'The Pulley' and then flicked over the pages and read 'Easter' and 'Virtue' and 'Discipline', and Patricia knew that at last she had met someone to whom she could speak her heart out and he wouldn't, like Blanche, think her mawkish because she said love straight out, or giggle, like Angela, that she was pious because she talked about immortality, or ask what did she mean? like Jimmy Windermere, if she mentioned anything that he couldn't see, couldn't hear, taste or feel. Patricia was, in fact, more intelligent than you would have suspected; more intelligent than she looked; too intelligent for her environment: all her life it had been only to her grandfather that she had been able to speak freely and he was old; he was disillusioned and had learned patience: wait, he said, we shall know it all one day; and, he said, you're not the first one, and, we must take life as we find it and, yes, change this and that, but human nature doesn't change. It was heaven therefore to talk to Hugh, to say, don't you hate resigned people? and, life's so easy if you know what you want and smash the half-gods; and, isn't it awful that some people live in slums and some in palaces? and, of course stupidity is at the bottom of everything: we must educate them . . . oh, clouds unfurl. Bring me my chariot of fire. When the train ran in to Norwich Station, they had not nearly finished their conversation and Hugh said, 'Look here, I'd like . . . I mean, don't you think we must meet again?' so Patricia, having discovered that his destination was a house under ten miles from Hulver, where he was to tutor a boy during the Easter holidays, invited him to lunch on the following Sunday. 'Will it be all right?' asked Hugh with nervous vagueness, and Patricia said, 'Of course. My grandfather loves having people.'

'But I mean, people you've met in the train?' said Hugh, bred in Peebles.

'What's wrong with the train?' asked Patricia, taking her dressing-case from him and catching the eye, as he never could, of a porter. 'You must meet somewhere.'

***

'Well, I'd love to come,' said Hugh and, 'Let me carry that,' he remembered.

'At half-past one,' said Patricia and gave up her ticket, grinned at him, said, 'Hullo, James, how are the horses?'

The dressing-case was taken from him and Patricia vanished into the depths of a shining brougham. 'So long,' she called to him and James said something in the language unknown to him in which men talk to horses, and the crest and the cockade and the smell of it all, the plutocratic smell of leather and polish and horses, rolled away.

Hugh took a station fly and drove five miles to the house of a retired Indian judge, who said, 'The devil you are!' when on Sunday morning he announced that he was lunching at Hulver. He had hired a bicycle in the village and he started in good time, rode very fast and arrived at the lodge gates too early. But he didn't know how long the drive was, so he rode on and, emerging suddenly from under the oaks, found himself practically on the terrace. It was only one o'clock but he couldn't hide now; there were people standing on the stone steps of the house and they were looking at him. Appalled by his earliness, by the size of the house, by the fact that Patricia had picked him up in the train and probably forgotten her invitation, he dismounted, mopped his face, dusted his trousers and wheeled his ramshackle bicycle between the fountains and the statues to the foot of the steps, where he propped it against an urn containing daffodils.

Lord Waveney was standing on the steps with the Rector, and, while Hugh was propping his bicycle, he hurried down saying he expected that Hugh was Lindsay. 'That's right,' said

Hugh and he barked his shin against a pedal and said that he hoped it was all right his turning up like this – Miss Crispin had said that it would be.

Lord Waveney said, 'Of course, of course,' and, looking oddly like Patricia, he grinned and said, 'She didn't forget, but, if she had, it wouldn't have mattered. There's always a joint on Sundays.' Then he made introductions and Hugh, somehow more at his ease since the joint had been mentioned, shook hands with the Rector and agreed that he'd had a lovely ride from North Moreton. 'Come in, come in,' said Lord Waveney, but, as he spoke, there was a clatter of hoofs and Patricia made that sudden dramatic entrance on the terrace. 'Ah,' said Lord Waveney in the voice he kept for her. 'Here she is, and, damn it, she's riding Black August.'

From the argument that followed Hugh gathered that the tall black horse had recently thrown a groom and Patricia had been forbidden to ride him. 'Oh, Grandfather, don't be so silly,' said Patricia. 'You know he hates that mutton-fisted Funge. He's as quiet as a lamb with me.' Lord Waveney gave it up and took the Rector indoors and Patricia fed Black August with carrots from her pockets and told Hugh that he had won the Grand National. Believing that she was joking, since you don't see Grand National winners every day, Hugh gave a non-committal chuckle, but later, sitting at table with iced melon on his Crown Derby plate and a golden shameless Rubens on the wall opposite him, he realised that Hulver was the kind of place where that kind of thing happened. He should have disapproved; he should have remembered how horrid luxury is, that horse-racing wrecks homes, that works of art should be placed in museums where all can see them and profit, that many a poor child would have been glad of his melon. But he didn't. There was a gold spoon between his fingers, a Chippendale chair beneath him, Waterford glass at his right hand; at the table with him sat that incredible trio, the bad old lord, the stiff great lady and the red-headed hoyden who rode a Grand National winner; the Rubens glowed; somewhere doves were cooing; on the terrace the fountains made music, faerie music, delicate, soporific and calm. There fell on him, on quick opinionative prize-winning Hugh, the spell of Hulver. Drunk with the wine that the *genius loci* brewed, he stepped, an unlikely True Thomas, into that faerie land.

Lord Waveney liked him, liked his sensitive hesitating manner, admired and was amused by his sound Scots priggishness, knew perfectly well how Patricia felt about him and approved because here, he thought, is a boy who won't get into debt, take to drink or run after women. In two of these respects Victor Langdale was already causing anxiety and though light-hearted Angela could be consoled by a diamond bracelet or a trip to Cannes, he didn't think Patricia could; she thought a lot of Virtue and not much of diamonds and smart hotels. Blanche, on the other hand, had no idea that Hugh meant anything to Patricia. Nobody had dared to tell her that Lord Windermere had proposed and been rejected, and it simply didn't occur to her to consider Hugh as a possible rival. He was nobody; he was learned; he hadn't any *savoir faire*, didn't ride, dance or shoot. 'I suppose,' she said afterwards to Patricia, 'you thought he would interest your grandfather?'

* * *

'Yes,' said Patricia.

'Well, you seem to have been right,' Blanche owned, 'since your grandfather has seen fit to invite him for a fortnight. But I hope this won't encourage you to pick up young men in trains – goodness knows whom you might get hold of.'

Hugh went to stay at Hulver when his pupil had gone back to school and the university term had not yet started. He didn't, as Blanche had expected, sit all day in the library talking bookishly to Lord Waveney: Patricia put him on a lady's hack and with his heart mostly in his mouth he went riding with her through the April oak woods and across the melancholy marshes. Then Blanche took fright. 'Is it wise?' she asked Lord Waveney. 'What is wisdom – σοφίαὰ or φρόνησις?' he replied. Blanche was routed and tried what she could do with Patricia. 'He's nobody,' she said; and she said, 'What a funny friendship – you and a smuggy little Scotch professor,' and 'Ought we to offer him bacon and eggs with his tea?' Patricia kept her Burne-Jones mouth shut, ordered sandwiches for two, and when, on a Monday morning, Hugh proposed to her in a hay loft, accepted him.

Then, though she hadn't been shy with Hugh, she seemed nervous about breaking the news to her family, so Hugh, who never turned his back but marched breast forward, brushed the seeds of the old meadow hay from his Norfolk jacket and went straight into the house and asked where he could find Lord Waveney. 'His lordship is to be found in the office, sir,' said the footman, and Hugh, intimidated by Sammy Funge in plush breeches into asking himself what there was to these Crispins, smoothed his hair and made his way across the

* * *

hall to the stark vaulted room where Lord Waveney conducted what Hugh considered to be his negligible estate business. He didn't panic till Lord Waveney, having called him his dear boy and said that Patricia had more sense than her sister, asked him his income. 'I get five hundred a year,' said Hugh, and he shoved his hand through his hair and said, 'I must say, it sounds hopelessly inadequate.' There was a pause while Lord Waveney drew squirls on blotting-paper, and pride and prejudice ran out of the soles of Hugh's shoes and he muttered, 'I must have been mad . . . it's impossible, isn't it?' But Lord Waveney only laughed and said that of course he meant to do the same for Pat as he had done for Angela, and he said – rather coarsely, Hugh thought – that it was high time the family bred some scholars. 'Don't worry,' he told Hugh. 'I'll get my lawyer down and we'll go into it. Angela,' he said, 'had twenty thousand'; and he drew some more squirls and said, 'I'm fonder of Patricia.'

Hugh stammered out his thanks – it wasn't until he got back to Glasgow and was waiting in the rain outside the station for a tram that he remembered how easy it is for rich men to be generous – and Lord Waveney went out to the stables and told Patricia not to be a moral coward but consented to follow her into the yellow drawing-room when he had counted a hundred.

Patricia found Blanche at her embroidery and blurted out, 'I've something awful to tell you.'

'Not your grandfather?' cried Blanche and boasted afterwards that it had been a premonition.

Patricia, beating her riding boots with her switch, said,

'No. Hugh and I have got engaged and Grandfather says we can be.'

Blanche made a stitch. 'And who is Hugh?' she enquired icily.

'Mr Lindsay, of course,' said Patricia.

'Have you gone mad?' said Blanche, snipping a thread with gold scissors.

'No,' said Patricia.

'Then you must realise that you can't possibly marry him. He's nobody. He's got no place. He's been brought up quite differently. I shouldn't wonder if he expected you to live in a house in a row and to use asparagus servers and a cruet. . . .'

'What's this about a cruet?' asked Lord Waveney.

Blanche said, 'Patricia tells me that she has got engaged to that Lindsay creature. I'm telling her that it's quite impossible. He's not really a gentleman.'

'Nonsense,' said Lord Waveney.

Blanche said, 'You know best, of course. I admit that his manners aren't bad, but who are his people?'

'A good Scots family, probably older than ours,' said Lord Waveney. 'And anyhow, Blanche, you should be the last person in the world to over-estimate gentility. Almeric was a gentleman but . . .'

'Please,' said Blanche. 'Not before Patricia.'

'Patricia's grown-up and *compos mentis*. She must have realised that he didn't make you a good husband.'

'Things like that,' said Blanche, 'are better not mentioned. I am sure that in his middle-class way Mr Lindsay would make a good husband. But it's the small things that jar – cruets and asparagus servers and ferns . . .'

'Patricia,' said Lord Waveney winking at his grand-daughter, 'isn't such a fine piece of porcelain that she can't stand a jar. If I were a woman, I'd sooner my husband kept a cruet than a mistress. Damn it, I'd sooner he helped himself to asparagus with servers than to whisky without discretion. I like Lindsay. I like him much better than I like Victor. I've given my consent to this marriage, Blanche, and I hope you will.'

'If that is so, I can hardly do otherwise,' said Blanche and, shutting her mouth like a rat trap, she began to stitch.

'That's splendid,' said Lord Waveney in an encouraging tone, and he turned to Patricia. 'Run along now and find your young man and tell him it's settled.'

Patricia ran and Lord Waveney, like a good soldier, remained behind to consolidate his victory. He suggested a pretty country wedding – Angela had been married in London – and he suggested that Blanche should take Patricia to stay in London for a fortnight and buy the trousseau.

'My advice would be of little use. I really have no idea what middle-class women need,' said the furious stitching woman.

'Come, come Blanche, don't be ridiculous,' said her father-in-law. 'Patricia will need exactly what Angela had – I shall be very much annoyed if you spend a penny less on her. I am sorry that you are disappointed, but I hope that you will not allow your feelings to spoil the poor child's happiness.'

'I have told Patricia what my feelings are. I shall not mention them again,' said Blanche stiffly.

He left the room more or less satisfied, but he didn't know what Blanche could make of not mentioning. Face to face with Hugh, she made no reference to the engagement but talked about the weather; she sipped her champagne without a smile or a word and persisted in addressing him as Mr Lindsay. Hugh said, 'Your mother doesn't seem to be pleased,' and, 'Have I offended Mrs Crispin?' and neither Patricia nor her grandfather had the courage to tell the truth. Patricia said, 'I've never been told properly but I believe she was unhappily married,' and Lord Waveney said, 'Poor Blanche, she backed the wrong horse and the Branksomes have always been rotten losers.' Hugh preferred Patricia's explanation, cornered Blanche and told her that he meant to take great care of her daughter. 'Really?' said Blanche and rang the bell for the footman to poke the fire up.

Hugh left next morning. He wasn't sorry to leave. Though he pitied Blanche for her unhappy marriage and consequently warped outlook, her silence and obvious suffering made him uncomfortable. As he travelled north, back to his cold clean lodgings, his hard word and economical living, the spell of Hulver faded. He'd done a mad thing . . . a mad romantic thing . . . Patricia would have a thousand a year . . . it would make such a difference . . . how on earth would they spend it? Still further north, that difficulty vanished to be replaced by another. She was a baron's grand-daughter. She was used to a huge house . . . footmen . . . hunting. How would she settle down to be an ordinary man's wife? Even with fifteen hundred a year, she'd have to keep an eye on the bills, curb the extravagances of servants. He'd been mad, divinely mad . . . oh, well, what did they say, his sages? One and all, in accents stern, passionate, hearty, melodious but all beloved, they approved of him. Love is best, they said; love is enough; give all for love. Let me not to the marriage of true minds admit impediment, they said, and the light of a whole life dies when love is done. He had never himself written any love poetry. His own scholarly sonnets dealt with incidents in mythology or the wrongs of oppressed peoples, but you can't live for literature and not hear the nightingale. He got out a pencil and a sheet of paper and an hour later decided that the sonnet was too portentous a vehicle, but, stuffing the blank sheet into his pocket as the train drew in between the squalid backyards of the stark Glasgow tenements, he realised that it was the only poetical form in which he could express himself. In fact, not until he was fifty and love had become passionless, static and quite proper, did he write that poem to Patricia.

While Hugh travelled north wondering if he'd been wise, Patricia went riding on a mare which she thought she would buy from her grandfather with money saved from her more than adequate dress allowance and give to Hugh as a wedding present; Blanche sewed and thought how tiresome her daughters were – there was Angela, now immersed in dull domestic plans for the baby that was coming and Patricia getting away with this smuggy disappointing marriage; and Lord Waveney drove out to pay a call in his new Mercedes, crashed into a timber wagon and died in the road, calling for Patricia.

When Patricia got back from her ride, Blanche, hysterical from excitement rather than sorrow, met her in the stable yard and roughly broke the news to her. 'There's been a motor accident and your grandfather's dead. I don't know what will happen. You won't be able to marry that man now – everything will go to your cousin Andrew.'

Patricia said, 'He can't be dead. He can't. Where is he?' and when they had convinced her that the one tragedy, in the face of which all courage, hope and human power are useless, had happened, the first thing she did was to telegraph to Hugh to come to her.

Hugh, of course, couldn't come. There was his work and the expense of the journey. Her command reminded him that there are difficulties ahead for ordinary men who are foolish enough to fall under spells and get themselves engaged to barons' grand-daughters, and he saved money and gave Patricia a piece of his mind by telegraphing curtly, 'Impossible. Writing.' Patricia, tearing open the envelope, expecting, 'Love and sympathy. Starting instantly,' was downcast till she remembered Lord Waveney saying, 'Patricia isn't such a fine piece of porcelain that she can't stand a jar.' Hugh was surprised and a little ashamed when he received by return of post a sweetly reasonable letter.

In a yellow hay wagon, drawn by Suffolk Punches and followed by the Grand National winner with an empty saddle, Augustus Roderick, twelfth Baron Waveney, jolted across the park to lie under the yews awaiting judgement among his forebears and tenants, and his will, drawn up when Almeric died, was read in the library. Hulver, as everybody had known, was entailed and went to Patricia's cousin, Andrew, who had arrived that morning from Paris, where for the last ten years he had represented a London firm of exchange brokers. There were legacies to servants and charities. For Blanche, the executors were instructed to purchase an annuity of fifteen hundred a year. Angela and Patricia had each a legacy of five thousand pounds.

The weeks that followed were a nightmare for Patricia. She had adored her grandfather and she missed him painfully. Her cousin Andrew, a boorish young man deeply interested in electricity, walked about the house and grounds alone, inspecting his inheritance; the late Lord Waveney had never taken the slightest interest in him and he saw no reason why he should take the slightest interest in the late Lord Waveney's relicts now. He dismissed many of the older servants, advertised the horses and announced his intention of having Young Shaun, the wolfhound, painlessly destroyed. Patricia offered to take Young Shaun to the vet in Norwich and took him instead to a game-keeper's cottage, but that was all she could do to frustrate the new Baron's activities, and daily she lived through heartrending partings with snuffling septuagenarians and wistful hunters. Hugh, for reasons that she had decided to respect, wouldn't come to her; Angela was forbidden by her doctor to travel, and Blanche, resentfully packing up to retire to her native Monmouthshire, where, at any rate, she would be someone, talked of money, money, money all the time. You couldn't get on without two servants, she said, a house-parlourmaid and a cook-general, and that would be bad enough, for the cook-general would have the dining-room to do before breakfast, and either the breakfast would be uneatable or the dining-room only half done.

And only two servants meant a small house, a pokey villa, probably a house in a row, but that was all they would be able to afford, of course, Patricia and that Lindsay creature with only seven hundred a year between them. 'If your grandfather had lived to see to your settlements, you might have had a tolerable little place out in Ayrshire, but, as it is, I'm afraid you'll simply have to live like the tradespeople.' Blanche wasn't a cruel woman but, even if Hugh had been a rich man, she would have been desperately anxious now to postpone the marriage: self-willed as a mule, she wanted Patricia to go to Monmouthshire with her, so that there would be someone in the house to talk and talk and talk to; later on, of course, before people began to say that poor Blanche Crispin couldn't get her second daughter off, Patricia might marry a man who had money and a nice place where it would be pleasant to stay.

Patricia was very much in love with Hugh but, raised in Arcady, she had thought of love as an idyll: she hadn't realised that in this mad world its consummation includes the purchase of saucepans, visits to servants' registry offices and ceaseless calculations of how far the beloved's income will go. Blanche made lists of what Patricia couldn't do without and Patricia sent them to Hugh. Hugh crossed out houseparlourmaid, dinner service for twelve, champagne glasses and canteen of dessert knives. Blanche said, 'There you see, Pat, the man's impossible. You must write – quite kindly, of course – and break off the engagement.'

Patricia went for a last long ride on Black August. She thought about house-parlourmaids, dinner services for twelve, champagne glasses and dessert knives; and she thought about Hugh and all the lovely things he had said to her and how mad he'd been to propose to her and how it wasn't of earth, this strange thing that was between them, couldn't be bought or learned or willed but came suddenly and often inconveniently from heaven, and how, if she denied it, it might never come again, never again though she met a thousand men, handsome as Paris, brave as Hector and eligible as Lord Windermere. And she thought about Blanche and of how wrongly she always chose; what fools her friends were; on what joyless pleasures and parade she spent her money; how she read *The Times* and not poetry; how she bought diamonds and rang the bell to have the curtains pulled across the stars. She rode home and wrote to Hugh that night, suggesting that they should be married secretly in London.

Hugh wrestled with his Presbyterian conscience, consulted Mr Pope, Mr Dryden and the Reverend John Donne, wrote that he hated deceit and bought a special licence. Patricia packed a suitcase, slipped out of the house on a dewy May morning, kissed Black August goodbye and arrived at Liverpool Street Station with a full heart and an empty stomach. Angela, frivolous and loyal, took charge of her, fed her, hooked her into a Paquin model and, in spite of doctor's orders, drove with her to a quiet church in the City. Hugh had taken the night train from Glasgow. He was conscience-stricken, nervous, distrustful of Angela, whom he thought much too smart for an expectant mother, and almost rude to poor kind stupid Victor, who acted as best man, provided a champagne luncheon at the Berkeley, drank the better part of the magnum himself

✹ ✹ ✹

and made vulgar jokes about newly married couples on the
way back. But slowly as the day wore on, his mood changed.
The old spell reclaimed him. Conscience wilted. He felt the
queer charm that made Victor lovable despite his stupidity.
He forgot that Angela's pearls would have bought shoes for
half the barefooted children in Glasgow. Victor had booked
a box at the Gaiety and Hugh, who had never sat in a box,
never watched a musical comedy and never wished to, drifted
through his wedding night like a man in a dream, lolling in
his brocade theatre seat, washing in a pink marble bathroom,
sharing a black lacquer bed with a baron's runaway grand-
daughter and only now and then wondering if this were really
Hugh Lindsay. . . .

CHAPTER THREE

Adapt Yourself . . .

I

David Augustus Lindsay was born in nineteen hundred and sixteen. Hugh was at Salonika. Patricia was staying with Blanche in Monmouthshire. Victor was in France and Angela was working in a canteen in Rouen. Emotionally life was easy. All men were heroes. Angela had forgiven Victor. Blanche had forgiven Patricia, and now proudly referred to Hugh as 'my Salonika son-in-law'. David Augustus, a strapping eight-pounder, was the generation whose freedom we were fighting for, the heir of the land fit for heroes to live in.

Giles Roderick Lindsay was born in nineteen hundred and nineteen. The war was over. In the land fit for heroes, butter cost three shillings a pound; eggs were fourpence each; champagne was two pounds a bottle; servants were not to be had and if by some miracle you found a villa to let, you paid a rent which before the war would have hired you a mansion. Blanche had had to give up subscribing to the Life Boat and the Young Men's Christian Association; to meet debts, taxation and death duties, Victor had sold Clove Park, would demolish Finlay Castle and was advertising Upholt Hall. To add to the discomfort of the situation, one's outlook on life had altered. For five years one had eaten oysters, drunk champagne, made merry at the Ritz and the Alhambra and Murray's because tomorrow one was practically certain to die. Now suddenly in the place of death and one's name on the war memorial and being remembered at the going down of the sun and in the morning, a drab future loomed ahead. Once again it was necessary to plan, strive, push aside, stamp down. Cunning got the job; courage had served its turn, could blow out its brains or stick its head into the gas oven. Now purses closed, faces hardened and jokes fell flat.

Hugh and Patricia found a ponderous villa inconveniently far from the University, for which they undertook to pay a rent of a hundred pounds a year. It stood on a slope, the front garden being banked up by a wall of red sandstone, glaringly overhung by aubretia and yellow alyssum, and its protruding plate-glass eyes stared angrily at a similar structure on the opposite side of the road. The front rooms were square and high and bleakly lit by large bow windows. The kitchen and scullery were dark; their windows were narrow and obscured by the high wall of the tradesmen's mossy entrance. The back garden was square. There was a lawn in the middle; a narrow path went round it, and there was a flower bed, three feet wide and badly needing manure, between the path and the wall. There were no trees in the garden but under the wall of the house shrubs hid drains. Patricia, remembering the oaks of Hulver, bought a standard apple tree and planted it on the lawn. It quickly died.

＊ ＊ ＊

The house was called 'Loch Lomond'. Hugh, possessed by a defence complex, saw nothing wrong with it. It was well built, he said. It was light and airy. The drains were in good condition. There were plenty of cupboards, he pointed out, a good sound slate roof and room in the hall for the pram. Nine-tenths of the inhabitants of Glasgow would consider it a palace, he said, and he said that Patricia must have known when she married him that he wouldn't be able to provide her with a house like Hulver.

Patricia, who had never heard of a defence complex, said, 'Oh, don't be so silly. *All beauty in a little room may be, though the roof lean and muddy be the floor*. I know that, Hugh. I never expected you to provide me – as you call it – with a house like Hulver. I don't want a house like Hulver. But don't you see – I shouldn't mind a hut or a tenement in the Gorbals or a disused railway carriage, but this place is smug; it's respectable; it's prosperous. . . .'

Then she learned something about Hugh. Though he was a scholar and a bit of a poet, he didn't mind being smug. He respected respectability. He yearned to be prosperous. Because he wasn't, because he hadn't a more gentlemanly house, well-trained maids, good carpets, a conservatory, large oil-paintings, a loaded sideboard, imposing meals, quite sub-consciously he was always alert to catch her grumbling and defend himself and score off her with some bitter phrase about the idle rich or marrying beneath you. 'Sorry I can't provide fountains,' he'd say if Patricia mentioned that it was hot in the garden, or if she reported a dull tea party, 'I'm afraid that in Glasgow we don't run to lords and ladies'; yet it was the builder's son and not the baron's grand-daughter who complained, 'The children aren't fit to be seen,' and, 'Are those all the cakes you've got to offer Mrs Montgomery?'

The large square rooms at 'Loch Lomond' had to be furnished, and with post-war prices obtaining, Hugh's war gratuity furnished three of them. For her bedroom Patricia bought the cheapest suite she could discover in Sauchiehall Street. It cost thirty guineas; it was constructed of oak-stained deal, and inside the wardrobe and wash-hand stand you could detect the trademark of a firm of sugar importers. Blanche had promised to give them some furniture. While she had lived at Hulver she had stored a quantity which she had inherited, and, on departing for Monmouthshire, she had supplemented this by the simple process of going round the house, observing, 'He won't want that', and marking whatever she fancied with her initials. The Monmouthshire house was choc-a-bloc with furniture but the selection which Blanche sent carriage-forward to Glasgow was disappointing. There was a varnished chest of drawers with three handles missing, a marble-topped wash-hand stand which wobbled, six chairs that needed caning, some framed water-colours executed at an early age by the donor, eleven croquet hoops, several large trunks, two pestles and mortars, a colossal knife-cleaning machine, a dozen copper jelly moulds, six thirty-foot damask tablecloths and a cracked commode. Hugh was offended and wanted to send the whole consignment carriage paid to the next jumble sale in Monmouthshire, but Patricia dissuaded him. She used the mortars as drinking bowls for Young Shaun, the wash-hand stand as a scullery table, tore up the damask tablecloths and used them to bandage grazed knees, had the chairs recaned and chopped the chest of drawers and the commode into faggots. For the first time in his life, Hugh overdrew his account and with many remarks about trusting in princes bought more furniture.

In those early years, he was a difficult husband. Poor but proud – so he thought – he was easily offended. His Scots reserve involved them in innumerable misunderstandings. He never said, 'I hate your having to cook and push the pram.' He said, 'It would have been better for everyone if you had learned to cook instead of learning how to break horses.' He didn't say, 'I wish I could afford to keep a horse for you.' He sneered at 'huntin', fishin' and shootin''. Though he must have known better, he persuaded himself into believing the handy old sophistry that women are adaptable and made no allowance for the fact that Patricia was tackling a job that she hadn't been born or bred or trained for.

'What *can* you do?' he asked her over a soggy beefsteak pie, and Patricia in tears said, 'I could hunt a provincial pack. . . .' and Hugh made his irritating contemptuous noise – pshaw, and said, 'My God, what a useful accomplishment!' Patricia was silent, and though it occurred to Hugh that if *he* were suddenly called upon to live the life *she* had been used to, he would make a remarkably poor job of it, he wasn't in those days sufficiently generous to say so. Instead he lectured her very kindly and sensibly, showing her what an empty and selfish life it had been, telling her how much more merit and gallantry there was in this job of making a comfortable home for a hard-working man and his children.

* * *

Patricia thought back. It didn't seem to her that her life at Hulver had been empty. There had always been something to do, a bazaar to organise, a young horse to school, new people to call on, a long way to walk with grapes and wine for an invalid. As for her grandfather, he had spent every morning in his office and most afternoons inspecting crops, timber, livestock, leaking roofs, smoking chimneys and over-flowing cess-pools. She said so, but Hugh said that wasn't work but insolent patronage. Patricia hadn't learned logic, economics or sociology, nor did she know that words and phrases are the leaves and brambles of the thicket hiding the well at the bottom of which Truth lies; Hugh could always silence and generally convince her; and he convinced her now. She dried her eyes, remembered who'd made her bed, and got down to the business of lying on it.

Hugh deplored her upbringing but, whatever she'd not learned, she knew how to ride at her fences. Next morning she got out of bed without the yawn which made Hugh say that she should have married a lord if she wanted nine o'clock breakfast, and, after speaking to the cook about beefsteak pies and receiving a week's notice, she went to the newsagent and cancelled her order for *Horse and Hound*, substituting *Woman and Home*. She set to work to study cookery books and dietetics. She learned to wash woollens. She made herself pleasant to the domesticated young wives of Hugh's col-leagues, swopped recipes and household hints and knitting directions. It wasn't easy. She had no method, no handiness. Inanimate objects seemed to conspire against her, saucepan lids falling on tumblers, broom handles poking through

* * *

window panes, milk boiling over, stews boiling dry, rice swelling, wool shrinking, stitches dropping, needles breaking, and all the time the old life calling, the smell of a new leather dog lead turning her sick for the feel of a horse under her, the south-west wind blowing indigo clouds across primrose sunsets till her heart ached with nostalgia for long rides home along dusky English by-roads. Then she'd think, I'm sick of it, or, God, give that hour back, or, quite frankly, I'd have done better to take Jimmy Windermere. But there were the children, sturdy August, grave Giles, and Nicola, the new enchanting nut-brown baby; for the beauty and the love and the fun and the hope that they were, this shortened step, these aching legs, this end to adventure was a small price to pay. She hadn't the mind that disdains the common round. Country-bred, she knew that the world could exist without kings but not without cowmen, and it hadn't been for want of trying that she'd made a soggy mess of a beefsteak pie. All the same, as she realised now, like Lot's wife she had been looking over her shoulder, looking back to Hulver; and she made up her mind only to look forward; and she gave up armchair hunting, and telling the children about Hulver, and teaching them hunting noises, and carrying carrots in her pockets.

And all the time, like a tide stealing out unnoticed, draining, furrowing, sucking, taking this and that, the months went by, and drunken Irish cooks succeeded one another in the dark kitchen, disappeared on their afternoons off or were expelled by Hugh; Highland nurse-housemaids wheeled out the children, pined and departed, explaining that the sickness was on them for Achnashellach or Glenuig. Patricia, cooking, sweeping, dusting, scrubbing, washing, pushing the pram, grew quick and competent, forgot the stillness of winter oak woods before a hound speaks, walked briskly past the saddler's thinking that if tomatoes were too dear she'd buy liver to cook with the bacon, talked of prices, talked of shops and servants, took a pride in her clean house, her neat mending, her well-balanced, well-cooked meals.

And Hugh saw that she had adapted herself. His beef-steak pies were no longer soggy. There were cakes for Mrs Montgomery. His socks were darned. He walked on polished linoleum and bright carpets. His children looked tidy in their grey flannel shorts and the neat well fitting jerseys which Patricia could knit so fast. It didn't occur to him to wonder whether she were dead or sleeping, the red-headed hoyden who had taken him riding in the Hulver oak woods; it didn't occur to him to ask whether it was at all painful, this adapting process, whether the young self whimpered as you smothered it deeper and deeper until it slept or died. He took for granted and sincerely loved the admirable helpmeet that life had broken for him. He forgot that she was Lord Waveney's grand-daughter and used to footmen, and his pride was soothed. He was cured of his defence complex and became a happy man.

II

August was twelve, Giles ten and Nicola six when Hugh's father died leaving an estate which, equally divided between Hugh and his two grim spinster sisters, added three hundred a year to his income. Patricia suggested leaving 'Loch Lomond'. She had taken a fancy to the old stone houses in Ayrshire, which stand with their backs to the moors and their feet in the waters of the Firth of Clyde. 'We could keep a pony for the children,' she said, 'and they could get handy in boats and learn to shoot and fish.' But Hugh didn't want his children to shoot and fish and ride ponies. He wanted them to have a first class education that would fit them for the struggle of life. Patricia knew now that life's a struggle and, though she didn't think all Hugh did of education, she was so accustomed to giving up things, that she agreed with scarcely a pang; and August and Giles were sent to a preparatory school in England. Hugh's three hundred covered the reduced fees generously allowed to brothers but did not provide for travelling expenses, dancing lessons, boxing lessons, blazers, sports subscriptions, subscriptions towards a new pianoforte, a new cricket pavilion, a new gymnasium and handsome wedding presents for junior masters, so Patricia dismissed the fairly satisfactory cook whom she had humoured through a couple of years, and undertook the whole work of the establishment. Hugh wasn't a slave driver, but he believed that hard work never hurt anybody, and now that the boys were away and Nicola a day boarder, Patricia, he felt, might just as well employ herself in pottering usefully about her own home as in gadding out to watch the illiterate muck that's shown at cinemas, or to play the soul-destroying game of golf, or to chatter chiffon and scandal over tea and sugared cakes with other idle women. He forgot the holidays when, annotating Beaumont and Fletcher, he asked for quiet

– nothing more; and there was the Easter when August had appendicitis and the Christmas when Giles had jaundice and the long and awful summer holiday by the white beaches and the jade green seas of Morar when Giles decided that it was cruel to fish, Nicola developed a mother fixation, and it only made August swim further and further out if you shrieked at him to be careful from the shore. Then Patricia, not really clever, not even sure how to spell psychology, had some more adapting to do. Now it wasn't cut knees, dirty necks, getting lost, getting run over that she must beware of; but it was worse things; it was quarrels and complexes, sulks and selfishness, getting narrow-minded, getting sentimental, answering Hugh back, mocking his sages, taking his scissors. Patricia's legs didn't ache so much now that there was no pram to push, but often she wished that the children were small again and that she was trudging down Sauchiehall Street pricing tomatoes with Giles dawdling, August running ahead and Nicola in the pram grabbing at the parcel of mince; for, though your legs ache, you can still go on walking, whereas tact, patience, wisdom are apt at any moment suddenly to forsake you. And Hugh was no help. He hadn't been any help when the children were little, couldn't play, was revolted by egg on bibs, wouldn't read aloud because children's books were such nonsense; but she had been sure that once they passed the nursery stage he would delight in their growing minds. But he didn't. He was impatient with ignorance, irritated by error, couldn't understand why August didn't enjoy doing Latin verses, was shocked and depressed because Giles preferred Newbolt to Milton. He was strict in those days, down

* * *

like a ton of bricks on OK or *tu quoque* and there was August grumbling, 'Can't we go out and *do* something?' and Giles wailing, 'Why *shouldn't* I read if I want to?' and Nicola weeping, 'I *know* you love August and Giles better than you love me.' Aching legs had never spoilt Patricia's sleep but wondering if she'd been wise did, and though her hair kept its flaming red, a furrow appeared between her eyebrows; she grew thinner, looked harassed and, though she still wore tweeds and brooches with foxes' masks on them, strangers never summed her up as an outdoor woman: where were her children at school, they asked at once, and did she dread whooping cough most or measles? And creasing her forehead deeper, Patricia would begin over again the story of August's tonsils and Giles' pneumonia, and it didn't occur to her that there had been a time when she hadn't dreaded anything. . . .

III

When August was sixteen and Giles fourteen and Nicola twelve, there came from Oxford the offer of a professorship for Hugh. He flicked the letter over to Patricia and went on eating haddock, though all the stars were singing for him, the shivering small boy who had gone in home-made clothes to school in Peebles. Patricia said, 'Oh, Hugh, how lovely!' and Hugh said, 'The move will be expensive,' and he said, 'It will mean a great change.'

'Oh, darling, don't be so *elderly*,' said Patricia, and Hugh said, 'We're middle-aged.'

✳ ✳ ✳

Patricia felt it. The boiler had burst on Christmas Eve; Giles was in bed with earache and the doctor had said that in three weeks he would be able to tell whether it were a mastoid abscess; Nicola was dissatisfied with her present from Auntie Angela, and August had announced that morning that there was nothing in this damned bloody hellish place to do. 'I know,' said Patricia, 'but it isn't as if it means a different kind of work. And the Oxford doctors are so good,' she said, thinking of Giles. 'And there must be lots of young people there,' she said, thinking of August. 'And Nicola,' she said, 'will be able to go to a good boarding school.'

'And how will *you* like it?' asked Hugh.

Patricia, thinking of Giles's ear, August's outburst and Nicola's habits of whining, hadn't considered that. She said, 'Oh, I shall be all right if the rest of you are.'

IV

Hugh proposed to live in Merton Street, where he'd hear the bells, hear the footsteps, see the shadows move across the cobbles and the red leaves drift and the wind in the scholars' gowns. He wanted to know all day and all night that he was in Oxford, that Hugh Lindsay, the builder's son with a running nose and broken chilblains, had got there. Patricia walked along Merton Street and thought it very charming but no place for dogs or children and was glad when she found that the house which she had come to look over was indisputably too small.

No other houses in the town were available except in

* * *

North Oxford, which Hugh barred, so Patricia, secretly rejoicing, looked further afield and found a derelict farm-house on the slopes of Cumnor Hill. It was an old house, whitewashed and holly-covered and insecurely roofed with moss-grown tiles. There was an orchard and a paddock and a meadow and a spinney and outbuildings – a stable and a cart-shed and a cow byre. Patricia looked over the house first and then she wandered into the yard, and a faint lingering smell of cows and horses came to her, and standing in the mud, fiddling with a pump that didn't work, she made up her mind to have her way for once, and live here.

Hugh was difficult. He said that there was too much ground and look at all those hedges always needing to be trimmed. Patricia pointed out that you layered hedges once in twenty years and then clipping them took no more time than you'd spend over the shrubs and ivy of the Merton Street house.

Then Hugh objected to the outbuildings and had to be assured that they had stooped up, however drunkenly, for two hundred years and weren't likely to collapse abruptly now. Then he shifted his ground and said that living so far out they would move in the wrong circles – get to know county people without an idea in their heads instead of his col-leagues' families. The fact was that in some corner of his mind he feared the place, feared that lingering smell of cows and horses, the lift of the newly turned plough behind the house, the sounds that blew down on the wind from the beagle kennels – it was Hulverish. He didn't realise that he was scared, that he distrusted the sounds and smells because

* * *

they were suggestive of a way of life he'd not been brought up to. He believed that he was being wiser than Patricia. He adored Oxford and he made up his mind that it would be so much nicer for Patricia to live in his city of dreaming spires among intelligent people and marvellous concerts and wonderful intellectual activities than out here among dripping trees, staring cows, bone-headed neighbours and yelping beagles.

They discussed the problem inconclusively for weeks and then they went to see the house again and took the children. August walked about saying nothing, but at the sight of the leaning cartshed and the dim brown stable his handsome inexpressive face took on a look of bemused contentment. Nicola, who liked change, rushed about approving of everything, but it was quiet Giles who won the day for Patricia. He stood at one of the windows and looked out and said breathlessly, 'It's Matthew Arnold', and by a lucky stroke of chance Hugh was in the same room and heard him and said, by jove, so it was. Giles went on to discover that on winter evenings from the window you'd be able to see 'the line of festal light in Christ Church Hall', and that settled it. Hugh bought the house and always stoutly denied that he had objected to it.

They moved south in the autumn. Hugh was one of those people on whom success falls like a blessing. With all his charm he had been prickly, didactic as men under the tyranny of an inferiority complex generally are. Success altered him. From among the brilliant and the wise, Oxford had chosen him to profess the poets, and the thing was proven – he had

51

no longer any urge to comfort his self-respect by domestic severities. He grew genial, bought August a gun, gingerly patted the neck of the aged hunter which was going to provide such healthy exercise for the children; he shut his eyes to the fact that August, hanging round the beagle kennels and putting up jumps in the meadow, was going all Crispin; he smiled gently, sipping his port, when Giles made out a case for the modern poets. He had reached his goal and Oxford possessed him. All passes, said the bells in the tall towers; and the feet of the young men whispered in the streets, and they weren't the first or the last young men, said the bells: gnash your teeth, tear your hair, write to *The Times*, abolish the School Certificate, but twenty years, thirty years, forty years hence there'll still be young men coming up from the river thinking they're gods because they're stroking an eight, climbing into college through lavatory windows thinking they're stout fellows, allowing the tobacconist's daughter to seduce them because they think they're men of the world. Take the long view, said the bells, and then it didn't matter much that August had abused his position as Head of his House by throwing a sherry party, or that Giles thought Auden a greater poet than Keats, or that Nicola couldn't open her mouth without uttering some Americanism. And, taking the long view, it didn't matter much that one man out of all the millions of men who had lived and been glad and suffered and all the millions who would live and be glad and suffer, hadn't the house he'd wanted, or sons as intelligent as he could have wished, or had frayed shirt cuffs, or was getting old, had a denture now, didn't feel inclined to make love to his

* * *

wife, had lost his taste for ice-creams and polemics. Hugh, once brisk and prize-winning, grew vague, tolerant, donnish, beamed on youth, suffered fools, stepped off pavements under the bonnets of motor buses. . . .

CHAPTER FOUR

We All Come to It

I

Little Mr Binney picked lightly, thinly, busily, like a fairy roadmender, thought Patricia, content to be sitting there with her red head on the green plush head rest and her hands in the lap of the grey homespun skirt, which she had forgotten to change but it didn't matter because Oxford was nearly as bad as Glasgow and she had come and would go in her mackintosh. It's fairy work, she thought, all dexterity, no heart or strength needed; and she didn't wonder that Mr Binney, picking lightly, thinly, busily, day after day, year after year in his moss green room in pale Beaumont Street, had grown sharp-nosed, desiccated, unsubstantial as a Rackham gnome.

Mr Binney, uttering a vexed 'Tch, tch', withdrew his bright thin instrument and, knitting his brow said as though Patricia were to blame, 'Well, Mrs Lindsay, it's no use patching *that* up again. The best thing we can do is to get rid of it.'

Patricia, who had been glad to shut her Burne-Jones mouth, opened it again to say, 'Oh dear! How tiresome!'

'I'll put a temporary dressing in now,' conceded Mr

Binney, but he continued inexorably, 'We'll make an appointment for early next week. It's Doctor Hill, isn't it? Of course it will mean a plate in the lower jaw.'

'Oh damn – I mean dear. How tiresome,' said Patricia.

Mr Binney flung wide the gates of his white enamel cabinet. 'Oh well,' he said. 'We all come to it.'

Oh well, echoed Patricia, we all come to it. Hugh's got a plate and lovely Angela's got a front tooth that screws in, and Mother's got complete dentures. We all come to it. I've always known that. We all come to it, but not me . . . not me. . . .

'Open,' said Mr Binney.

He packed Patricia's mouth with cotton wool and inserted into the decayed tooth his Lilliputian dressing. 'You've got such a small dental arch,' he complained. 'It makes everything twice as difficult.' He blew hot air on the dressing, removed the cotton wool and handed Patricia a glass of purple water.

Patricia swilled her mouth out and rose. Mr Binney said, 'Don't bite on that tooth,' and rang the bell.

'Monday and Tuesday are no use,' said Patricia.

'We must make it Wednesday then,' said Mr Binney as the doctor's widow, who was his receptionist, carried in his appointment book. He ran his finger down a page. 'Wednesday, at eleven.'

'All right,' said Patricia. 'Eleven. Wednesday. Thank you. Goodbye.'

She went out. The receptionist closed the door behind her. Mr Binney returned to his cabinet, replaced this and that and threw the instruments he had used into the steriliser, thinking, Mrs Lindsay doesn't like the idea of a plate; it's wakened her up to the fact that she's getting on, and quite time too – with that great undergraduate son of hers she must be well on the wrong side of forty. All the Lindsays were patients of Mr Binney's and he disliked them all. He disliked Hugh because he forgot his appointments and, when he did come, inadequately excused himself by obscure quotations from eighteenth-century poets; he disliked August because, after all our efforts to educate the young into regarding war as a crime, he was going into the army; he disliked Giles because he didn't speak but only blinked, and Nicola because she didn't laugh at the jokes which amused other children. And he disliked Patricia because he was always seeing photographs of her sister in the *Tatler*. Mr Binney, like many insignificant persons, was hard to please.

Patricia pulled on her hat, buttoned her mackintosh and stepped out into pale Beaumont Street. The day had been wet. It was raining still and dusk had fallen early, but that wasn't as depressing as it would have been a week or two ago, for the shortest day was over: once again you could look forward to the spring. But what's the use of spring to me, thought Patricia. It'll be light after tea and, as I go down the garden to get the eggs, a blackbird will sing in the holly; the chestnuts will flower in Christ Church meadow and Magdalen will have her fritilleries, but I'll have a beastly dental plate . . . I'm old . . . Hugh's old. God! what a struggle it's been, she thought, catching the Botley bus by the skin of her teeth at Carfax, finding a seat, slumping down, remembering monthly nurses, infant diarrhoea, sticking out teeth, tonsils, tempers, name-tapes, rows about dirty necks, rows about reports, rows about tidying up the nursery; and now that I've finished with it, she thought as the bus rattled down Queen's Street, now that they're grown-up, wash themselves, feed themselves, take themselves there and back, don't quarrel any more or drop egg down their fronts, now that my work's done, I've just got to grow old and feeble and ugly. And what then? she asked, passing the marmalade factory, diving under the bridge, fleeing on between the lighted dolls'-houses, and answered herself: some foul disease – a paralytic stroke and your face all sideways, or cancer and your last words on earth a howl for morphia; and then at the lunatic bidding it's best to make a God of, the silver cord loosed and the golden bowl broken and behold! in spite of your pride and your fuss, it had all been vanity. For all it mattered, you might never have existed, who were 'just one insect the more, born of the heat to hum beneath these lovely skies'. . . .

The bus stopped at the Ferry Hinksey footpath and Patricia got out and switched on her torch. Walking across the meadows between the willows that were gaffers in the pale beam she shone on them, she could see the lights of Hodson's Pightle under the dark hump that was Cumnor. She was cold. She was miserable. She was hungry. She wished she were at home now – there would be eggs for tea because Giles had been for a long walk and August and Nicola had been beagling. And suddenly with the eye of her mind she saw the children as she would see them presently when they were sitting round the table, fair August, dark Giles and nut-brown Nicola. Oh well, she thought, if you've got children, what does it matter if you grow old? If my teeth fall out, Nicola's teeth are like peeled almonds. I've forgotten what it's like to ride, but there's August with a seat on a horse that ninety-nine men out of a hundred would envy. I can't risk my neck, but Giles means to risk his on Everest.

She stepped into the ferry boat, which, thank goodness, was on the right side, and pulled herself hand over hand on the wire rope across the dark water. The water rippled at the bow and reminded her of summer and how the children loved the river and how well they swam and how lovely they looked, naked and wet and honey-brown in the sunshine. Oh well, when she's too old even to bathe she'll watch them swimming – already when people say how well August rides it's even better than when hounds found in Hulver woods and ran to North Moreton and she was there, at the kill, a child of twelve on little grey Charity. . . .

She walked up the lane and through the gate into the hayfield. It had been awful having them . . . she had had heartburn with August, shingles with Giles and piles with Nicola, and it had been worse – her back had ached, her legs had swelled, she could have screamed with nervous exhaustion washing their bottles, spooning food into them, pushing them in prams. But you only had to wait, carrying on, putting one foot before the other quite blindly, and the pattern resolved itself, the muddle and the mess were over, and there was the pattern that the prophet, who wrote Ecclesiasticus and was obviously childless, hadn't seen, but another had seen, who had written the words she had once thought heartless but now found so comfortable: *Instead of your fathers you shall have children, whom you shall make princes in the land.*

She opened the gate at the top of the hayfield and walked up the steps to the terrace. The french windows of the dining-room opened on the terrace, and she went in and saw by the firelight that the tea was set on the table and the electric kettle was on the boil. The children must be starving, she thought, but it's like them to wait for me.

She stood in the dining room and shouted, 'Oy!' The schoolroom door opened with violence and there they stood with their heads among the Christmas decorations, August and Giles and Nicola, her princes in the land.

II

'Did he hurt?' asked August, cutting bread for everybody.

'No,' said Patricia, grasping the teapot. 'He only put in a temporary stopping. But I've got to have it out on Wednesday.'

'Oh, poor you,' said August.

'Gas?' asked Giles.

'Shall I go with you?' suggested Nicola.

They were sympathetic. They weren't like the Cliftons, who rushed about in cars all day and when they came in for their meals never asked what their mother had been doing. She beamed on them. 'It's all right. I'm used to it. How did you get on?'

August said, 'Hadn't someone better call Daddy?'

'He must have heard us,' said Patricia.

'Not if Mr Dryden and Mr Pope are with him,' said Nicola.

She went out munching. She was sixteen, a tall thin creature with a grave face, straight nut-brown hair and eyes of the same colour with stars in them. Though she had a fancy for black sequin dresses, Patricia persuaded her to wear brown or green, and she looked like a child of the woodlands, enigmatic and withdrawn.

'It was lovely,' said August. 'The woods were wild and wet and purplish.' He paused, screwing up his eyes, seeing it again and Patricia had time to feel glad that August, who wasn't clever like Giles or intelligent like Nicola but only kind and charming and handsome and rather gallant, had this love of beauty. Is it because when he was little in Glasgow I showed him the right things, she wondered; pointed out cranes against the sunset and trams like schooners and lights in the water? Or would he have been the same if I'd told him which was the live wire and how many tons the cranes could hoist and where the electricity was generated? I think I gave him beauty, she thought. In a dull home he might have been a dull boy; and Giles merely sharp and Nicola just an ordinary schoolgirl, all her charm lost if she were dressed wrong. . . .

August said, 'We drew the spinney behind the farm for ages and we were going over to the big wood when a hare got up in the cabbages. We had ten minutes over plough, which was awful – I had half Oxfordshire on my shoes – and then we checked at the cottages. Oh, it was superb,' he said, tilting back his chair and laughing. 'A hag came out of one of the cottages and went for Nicola, waving a broom and saying hadn't she anything better to do than to chase poor dumb animals.'

Giles said, 'I don't blame her.'

✳ ✳ ✳

August only grinned at that, and Patricia thought, thank goodness, I've taught them to be broadminded. It's not in every home Giles could say that . . . he'd have to prevaricate, even go beagling with the others, but I've taught them tolerance; they speak their minds without fear . . .

'Hullo,' said Hugh coming in behind Nicola, wearing the dazed look of a scholar abruptly yanked back from another century. 'So the hunters are home from the hill. How did you get on, Patricia? The dentist, wasn't it? Did he hurt you?'

'No, not a bit,' said Patricia, thinking, I'll tell him presently . . . no, I won't. I'll buy another toothglass and at night they can go into the medicine cupboard. . . .

August went on, 'We found again behind the cottages, and there we were all tied up in the hag's hen runs. By the time we got out and up on the hill, we were hunting at least six different hares. We spent the rest of the afternoon whipping in. God! I'm stiff.'

In Glasgow Hugh had never allowed his children to swear, but here in Oxford he merely wondered if it were just a passing fashion or a manifestation of the helplessness of youth, the cheep of the fledgling newly emancipated and subconsciously yearning for some maternal breast.

'Stiff?' said Patricia pouring out second cups. 'My dear, what about tonight?'

'Tonight?'

'Yes, tonight, darling. Isn't it tonight that you're taking Elspeth Cameron to the Cliftons' dance?'

'Oh, yes, of course,' said August, and his fair face flushed to a deep crimson.

* * *

Oh, bother, thought Patricia. That's Giles and Nicola. They've been teasing him about Elspeth and it's really rather common of them. After all, he's one and twenty; he wants someone to think about when it's spring or the band plays *The Blue Danube*, and Elspeth's nice; she's pretty enough and she rides well and she has been known to read a book and she likes me. I'd like it to be Elspeth, thought Patricia, and, making it easy, she said, 'I suppose you'll be taking the car?'

'Yes, please,' said August.

'How many more parties have you got? I believe you've been out every night this week,' said Hugh, who even now had not quite got rid of theories held in pink sandstone villas on the outskirts of Peebles, theories that gaiety's wrong and that if you're not in by ten, you're up to mischief.

'There's a lull next week,' said Patricia, thinking with pleasure of the many invitations that the children had had this Christmas. People like them, she thought. They dance well and they're good-mannered. Even when they were small, the boys filled up their programmes and danced all evening and didn't slide on the floor or stand stuffing in the refreshment room. And Nicola, though she's silent, is decorative. 'Well,' she said, 'I've finished. What about the hens?'

'I've done them,' said Nicola.

'And the horse?'

August had brought Griselda in.

'And the Webbed Feet?'

Giles had done the Webbed Feet and fed the ferrets.

'Well, let's move,' said Patricia.

She got up and, followed by Hugh, went across the hall

into the library. It was a long room with windows to the south and west. The house was L-shaped and the dining-room and the small drawing-room had the view over the water meadows to the towers and spires of the town. Hugh had let the fire out, but the room was airless and hazy with tobacco smoke. Every table was littered with papers. The cover of the typewriter and a pile of eighteenth-century poets were on the floor.

Hugh looked round. 'If we're going to sit in here tonight I'd better tidy up a bit.'

'I shouldn't bother,' said Patricia, kneeling down to mend the fire. 'I shan't be sitting much, anyway. Nicola's going to a Pony Club rally tomorrow. I shall be cleaning tack in the bathroom.'

'Oughtn't the children to clean their own tack?' suggested Hugh.

'They do sometimes,' said Patricia. 'But you know what children are.'

Hugh stood for a moment packing his pipe slowly and scientifically. He'd been a child himself, he thought, so he ought to know what children were, but he had been so different – an ugly little Scots type he'd been, rigged out in home-made garments, his hands raw with broken chilblains, his head crammed with school-work, his heart sour with ambition, so different from August and Giles. At Giles's age, Hugh had been awkward, opinionative, self-conscious, class conscious, terrified of lords and workmen, terrified of women; and with the intention of helping his sons through the difficulties of adolescence, he had been careful to keep alive the memory of those miserable and mistaken days. But August and Giles didn't need his help. They had no difficulties. Their manners were delightful. With the same simple friendliness they talked with dons and dustmen, girls in shops and girls at dances, deaf relations, famous authors, farm labourers, preparatory schoolboys and babies in prams. At Hodson's Pightle there wasn't a subject you couldn't mention. There were no lady dogs, necessary articles of furniture, delicate states of health, or things that you would understand when you grew older. Patricia had her grandfather's liking for calling a spade a spade. It was impossible that these unintimidated outspoken boys could have anything in common with the muddled and mismanaged oddity that he had been. Like burns coming down from the hills, they were, clear as crystal, while he, poor little devil, had been the dark polluted ditch that crawls through a town. . . .

He lit his pipe with one of the spills that Nicola obligingly made for him. His thoughts had gone too far to form a coherent answer for Patricia, so he said nothing as he sat down at his desk and with a sigh took up the proofs that he was correcting. They were galley proofs of the American edition of his book on the Life and Times of Alexander Pope, and, though they had only arrived from New York that morning, they were already in a state of indescribable confusion.

Patricia watched him for a moment. He looked old, she thought, sitting there so quietly at the table, old and dry and scholarly. And he'd nothing to say, who had said such lovely things once; his mind had grown as quiet and set and old as his body. Life would be dull, she thought, my God! it would be

* * *

dull if it wasn't for the children. She picked up her knitting –
a yellow pull-over for Giles – and wondered what August
would look like in a scarlet mess-jacket.

III

August and Giles and Nicola had gone back to the schoolroom. Giles had wound up the gramophone and was playing
a Stravinsky record. Nicola sprawled on the sofa reading.
August sat on the battered nursery fireguard smoking a
Russian cigarette.

It wasn't much use, he thought, starting anything. Tea had
been so late that in half an hour he'd have to start dressing.
Damn it, he thought, it was idiotic to dress for dinner at the
George and the flicks, but, if he didn't, it would be perfectly
obvious to everybody that he wasn't going to a dance in North
Oxford with Elspeth Cameron. That had been a bloody silly
story to put up, he thought; he could have avoided the
dressing problem by saying that he was taking Elspeth to
the Cinema, but there it was . . . he'd always been a nervous
liar . . . look how he'd blushed just now when Mummy had
said what about dancing? Well, it was their own fault. You
couldn't tell parents things. His were broad-minded or
thought they were – anyhow, they prided themselves on
it – but they were parents. They wouldn't cut him off with a
shilling, probably they'd say very little, but all the same it
would be unspeakably awful, he'd feel bloody, if they found
out about Gwen. And supposing Giles and Nicola heard of it?
They wouldn't be shocked, of course, but they'd be critical.

✱ ✱ ✱

They'd laugh at her scarlet nails and incredible eyelashes. They'd imitate her refined accent. They wouldn't understand how, though she was as common as they're made and hadn't an idea in her head, she was the most exciting thing that had ever happened to him, so exciting that there wasn't a thrill left in anything else, not in beagling or riding or any of the things he'd been so keen on last Christmas holidays. It was all very well to say that you shouldn't tell lies, but you had to. In a world of saints, it would be quite easy to be saintly but people couldn't understand. . . .

'*Must* you play the gramophone?' said Nicola.

'I must,' said Giles.

Nicola sighed, stuffed her fingers in her ears and went on reading.

August pitched the end of his cigarette into the fire.

'I hope to God the bathwater's hot.'

'I shouldn't think so. Nicola and I both had baths when we came in,' said Giles.

August said, 'There'll be hell for someone if it isn't.'

He went upstairs and anxiously felt the pipes in the bathroom. The water was hot enough but not boiling. Damn, he thought, damn Giles and Nicola. Still, they're not bad, he thought, going into his bedroom and collecting his sponge, clean underclothes and dressing-gown. They're nicer than I am now . . . damn Gwen, he thought, I was like they are before I met her. God! I was young. I thought it was so simple. I thought you just went on as usual till you fell in love with someone like Elspeth and then, when you could afford to marry, you married her. But it's not simple at all, he thought,

✳ ✳ ✳

going back to the bathroom, turning on the hot tap and clouding the water with a handful of his mother's geranium bathsalts. It's not simple at all. It's so damned complicated that you can go to bed feeling a worm about it and wake up feeling as pleased as a peacock. I wonder what my father was like when he was young, thought August, letting himself gingerly down into the water that was too hot but wouldn't be hot enough if he ran any cold into it. I don't suppose he ever looked at a girl before he met Mummy. A marvellous lot, that war generation, he thought, before they turned bitter – went to war with Rupert Brooke and came back with Siegfried Sassoon, somebody said of them. I wonder how I'd do, he thought, soaping his neck, if there was another war and I was in it?

August gave up soaping himself and lay back in the now comfortably hot water. 'The King has been graciously pleased to approve of the grant of the Victoria Cross to Lieutenant (now Captain) David Augustus Lindsay. . . .'

CHAPTER FIVE

They're Parents

I

Giles had forgotten about the Pony Club rally and before Nicola was out of bed he had turned Griselda into the paddock. Nicola had spent half an hour catching her. Griselda had rolled and that had meant ten minutes grooming. Nicola was late and she felt hot and bothered as she jogged down the lane on her way to Cumnor.

Griselda was looking for trouble. She arched her neck and swished her tail and snorted at the idle cows behind the hedges. Nicola knew that at the end of the lane she would swing round and make for home or, if you checked her, would stand there for five, ten, fifteen minutes, dancing. It was all very well for Mummy to say, 'Use your legs,' but if you used your legs, Griselda went up to the moon and you might or might not go with her. Damn it all, why do I have to ride? thought Nicola.

It was only lately that she had realised that she didn't like riding, that she never had liked it. She wasn't nervous, but it simply bored her: Griselda was so tiresome and the pace so slow. Cars were different. You didn't have to go out with a bowl of oats, coax them, scold them, lead them in and spend another quarter of an hour saddling and bridling them. You went out to the garage, got in, pressed a button and you were off and there was no more bother, no exasperating battle of wills awaiting you at the end of the lane. Away you went! It didn't matter if you met traction engines or there were tar barrels, sacks or even cardboard boxes in the hedges. The blessed engine obeyed you. It had no moods or fancies. Fast or slow as you wished it, it took you where you wanted to go.

Then, damn it all, why do I have to ride? thought Nicola. It's simply because Mummy's mad on horses, so mad that she even called her first child after a horse – all very well to say that Augustus was after her grandfather and that David was what they meant to call him, but he was called after that silly old National winner in the end. She's mad on horses and for some insane reason people always expect their children to be like them. She wanted to have horsey children, and the wish was father to the thought, and, without ever asking us, she takes it for granted that we're horsey too. 'My children adore riding. . . .' 'My children hate machinery.' That's what she says to other people's parents, and she's said it so often that for years it never occurred to me to wonder if it were true. But now I've got a mind of my own, thank God. I've come out of the trance. I hate it. I hate it. When I'm grown-up I shan't ride ever. I shall get a job driving cars. . . .

Cars . . . cars. Nicola saw them – long low scarlet MGs to dash about in; colossal white Bentleys to roll across continents:

dark suave Rolls Royces to glide in the streets of capitals – and there she was, jogging along the lane at four miles an hour on the back of a stupid fanciful animal. 'Get on, you fool,' shouted Nicola, as they reached the top of the lane and Griselda began dancing.

Griselda had jogged up the lane thinking of nothing in particular, but when she reached the turn and knew that she must go out on the highroad, her mind's eye gave her a delicious vision of a certain patch of particularly sweet grass under the damson tree in the paddock. Better to be in the paddock eating than on the highroad not eating . . . Better safe in the paddock than all alone on the highroad between the dangerous hedges. Griselda felt all alone when Nicola or Giles were riding her. With August she wasn't alone. He was with her.

Not on, not on, she thought; home to the paddock; and because Nicola's strong but uncommunicative hands wouldn't let her swerve, she backed; back and back she danced nearly into the ditch, but the ditch was better than the lonely and dangerous highroad. 'Get on, can't you,' scolded Nicola in a voice that Griselda heard but it didn't talk to her; and a sharp kick came on either side of her ribs so suddenly that she jumped forward. Oh well, now that she had started she might as well go on . . . perhaps it would be all right even though she was alone. She was a clever horse and if she kept her eyes open she could jump away from the bad things in the hedges. . . .

'Thank God,' said Nicola as Griselda walked warily into the highroad, and she wondered gloomily how many more times she would have to ride this damned horse up that damned lane to a damned rally. Dozens of times, I expect, she thought; and every time Mummy will come fussing round to see me off, beaming and thinking what a nice treat for Nicola. Why can't I tell her? It's so silly, thought Nicola; the world wouldn't end if I told her. All that would happen would be that she'd have to stop saying, 'My children adore riding,' and, 'My children hate machinery.' Why can't I tell her? She prides herself on being broad-minded. She wouldn't say much to me. Probably she'd say, 'I'm glad you told me.' Oh, well, I suppose it's because she's a parent and you can't tell them things. However decent they are, you just can't tell them. Perhaps Griselda will die, thought Nicola, only that would be no good because Mummy would go without clothes or food or something and buy us another. It's no use, she thought despairingly. For years and years I shall have to go on riding. . . .

Patricia passed her on the highroad. The engine was missing badly, thought Nicola, and Mummy wouldn't have noticed it. What was spent on Griselda's oats, she thought, would go a long way towards buying a decent car instead of that old Tin Lizzie.

Patricia drew up, wound down the window and said, 'How's she going?'

'Oh, all right,' said Nicola.

Griselda stopped too, and put her nose like grey velvet through the car window. Patricia said, 'Darling!' and wished that she were sixteen and had Christmas holidays and didn't know the price of cod and didn't care if the cook's face

✳ ✳ ✳

registered displeasure and was riding a grey mare to a Pony Club rally. But that was only for a moment. Then she remembered how everything gets stale if you cling to it. . . . Don't cling but go forward and instead of your fathers you shall have children. . . . She smiled at Nicola sitting up straight, heels down, hands low and heart, of course, high; said, 'Darling!' this time meaning Nicola, let in her clutch, and, crashing her gears, drove on towards the town.

II

It was a fine morning. Wonderful weather for the time of year, said the shop assistants, reaching for soup, slicing rashers, grinding coffee, snipping through wire netting, matching darning wool. More like April than December, replied Patricia, in her grandfather's style, hail-fellow-well-met with everybody; and, as she jay-walked back to the car park, lugging her frayed basket, she called out, 'Hullo, lovely, isn't it?' to dons' wives cycling down from North Oxford with earnest faces just discernible between mushroom hats and Fair Isle mufflers. She didn't notice how faintly came the echo, 'Isn't it?' She didn't know that, while Hugh was thought charming in Oxford, she was disliked because she countenanced blood sports and had a son who had a fancy to die for his country; poor Patricia, raised at Edwardian Hulver, respected brains, didn't realise that the prejudices of Colonel Blimp are nothing when compared to the prejudices of the intelligensia. . . .

She dumped her basket in the back of the car and settled herself in the driving seat, glad that she was going home, that

* * *

the weather was fine, that cod was cheaper, that Nicola was having a nice time at the Rally, that August had had a nice time last night, that Giles had gone for a nice walk instead of stuffing over a book, that the funny noise the car had made on the way in didn't, apparently, mean anything. She started the engine and was about to move off when a small red sports car backed into the space beside her. She recognised the car and put her head out of the window.

'Hullo, Elspeth!'

Elspeth Cameron, accompanied by a Sealyham terrier, got out of the sports car and came to Patricia's window. She was fair, short and healthy. Her small well-chiselled nose was powdered with freckles; she had a wide well-shaped mouth, which was cheerful in repose, and a pair of long-lashed grey eyes, which Patricia likened to the luminous water of lakes in winter dusks. She usually dressed in shabby tweeds, to which hayseeds clung and the white hairs of her terrier, but at parties and when she went to London she smartened herself up, used lipstick and a vivid nail varnish. But her look of honesty and health persisted, penetrating eye veils and sequins, and no matter how she was dressed it was instantly apparent that she was, as Giles had disdainfully described her, 'a nice girl'.

'Hullo, Mrs Lindsay,' said Elspeth. 'You've finished early. Mummy's given me a list yards long and it's eleven o'clock already.'

Patricia said, 'Oh, poor you! The shops are crowded. I rose early like the virtuous woman. But then I wasn't dancing. Did you enjoy it?'

Elspeth looked puzzled.

'Enjoy what?'

'The dance last night.'

'Oh, was there one? Where? I wasn't asked. I must be "getting on" or "going off" or something.'

'Oh,' said Patricia, confused. 'I thought . . . I mean, I thought August was taking you . . .'

'No, worse luck,' said Elspeth. 'I darned my stockings.' She grinned at Patricia and said, 'There must be Another.'

'Oh no,' said Patricia hurriedly. 'I'm sure there isn't. I must have made a mistake. I often do, you know . . . all this house-keeping.' She let in the clutch, called 'Cheerio!' and sailed out into St Giles' without looking in her mirror.

A car hooted furiously and swerved past her.

She collected her wits . . . get into the middle and signal that you're going to turn right . . . drive down Beaumont Street . . . signal that you're turning left . . . perhaps it's nothing . . . perhaps it's something that you'll laugh at presently . . . often your knees shake and then it's nothing. . . .

But August, you idiot! You're twenty-one; you should know by now that luck doesn't favour liars, that I was sure sooner or later to run into Elspeth and ask how she had enjoyed the dance. Such a futile story you told us, and it's not fair . . . we've never laughed at you, criticised or objected . . . it must be something beastly, some hell of a mess, or you wouldn't have needed to lie to us. Is it a girl, thought Patricia, exceeding thirty miles under the railway bridge; some wretched platinum blonde from the town . . . ? but that isn't like August; he's always laughed at that kind of girl and liked honest-to-

✻ ✻ ✻

God country ones like Elspeth. Oh, bother, thought Patricia, doing forty-five down Botley Road, perhaps it isn't anything like that; perhaps we've been tactless, asked him where's he's off to and what he's been doing and he just wants to feel independent. But he didn't come back till after one, she remembered; and he couldn't have spent all that time drinking beer at Godstow or driving about the country in the car. Oh dear, it must a girl, thought Patricia, and that means that August isn't . . . well, isn't August, but one of the young men one reads about in novels and doesn't believe in. Perhaps it hasn't gone far, she thought, turning up the lane to Ferry Hinksey. Perhaps he's only taken her to the Cinema and held her hand. August wouldn't go farther, she thought. He wouldn't fall in love with her. She wouldn't have an idea in her head: she'd say get along with you and pardon, and without being in love with her he wouldn't make love to her . . . not August . . . he wouldn't be like the young men in novels. And where do I come in? she asked herself. Ought I to tell Hugh or ought I to say something to August? Hugh would be shocked; even if it wasn't a girl, he'd be shocked because August lied to us, and, if it was a girl he'd be horrified . . . he'd come all over Peebles. It would be better to say something to August, she thought, driving in through the gate, only finding out things is so awful . . . so vulgar . . . so hateful. Oh damn it, thought Patricia, pulling up and switching off the engine, I was so happy till this happened and I believe I'm really being idiotic. Can't a man take a girl to the cinema without telling his mother? Yes, she thought, sitting there staring in front of her, I'm making a mountain out of a molehill. It's tiresome.

It's silly of August to tell lies. Perhaps it's all rather funny. I'll ask Elspeth to dinner next week and perhaps she'll wear that blue frock of hers and take his mind off his Flossie. . . .

As she got out of the car August came from the kitchen door carrying a stable bucket. He was wearing riding breeches and a fisherman's jersey, which he had bought in Cornwall last summer. He carried the heavy teak bucket brimful without effort. Patricia was always touched to see his strength – once he had been so little – but today she told herself severely that there was nothing touching about it: everything was small and grew up, horses . . . hens . . . worms . . . and even cabbages.

She followed August into the stable.

'Today's good deed,' said August setting down the bucket.

'So you're up at last,' said Patricia.

'Yes,' said August. 'And while you've been enjoying yourself, I've spring-cleaned the stable.'

'It looks lovely,' admitted Patricia, looking round her. August had brushed down the cobwebs and cleaned the window. Golden straw, knee-deep awaited Griselda. The haybag was filled. There was a feed of oats in the manger.

All the same she said, 'I met Elspeth in Oxford.'

August picked up a pitchfork and stirred the bedding. There was a desperately anxious note in his, 'Oh, really?'

Patricia made the mistake of looking at him. She saw the brown back of his neck and the golden hair that grew low on it; she saw the line of his smooth flushed brown cheek and his absurdly long black eyelashes. Oh, he might be twenty-one and eleven stone ten and six inches taller than she was, but always to her he'd be a child, helpless, vulnerable. It was beastly of her to have found him out, to have tramped in, safe and grown-up, on his muddled little secrets. 'Yes,' she said and then, 'I forgot at the time – I meant to ask her to dinner.'

'When?' said August leaning on the pitchfork.

'Friday, I thought. If there's anything decent on, you could take her to the cinema.'

'All right,' said August.

Patricia went away into the house and August lit a cigarette and sat down on the corn bin. God! he'd had a fright. When she'd said, 'I met Elspeth,' her voice had seemed definitely accusing. But anyhow, he thought, resting his head against the wall and attempting a smoke ring, all's well that ends well . . . awful it would have been if she'd rushed up to Elspeth saying chattily, 'How did you enjoy the dance last night?' I must be more careful, he thought, and he thought, it'll be a blessing when term starts, though God knows I don't feel like settling down to Applied Tactics. A thrill tingled through him as he realised that there was only a fortnight to get through before term started and that there was an excellent way into St Mary's over the wall of the Warden's garden, and that last night, Gwen had practically promised. . . . Driving home alone, of course he'd panicked, shied like a horse at a fen. . . .

The gong rang for lunch and August got up and stretched himself. God! it was nice to be young and strong with all the adventures in the world in front of you. '. . . *Not while the light is dim but now from the heart of joy* . . .' Oh well, said August to his Creator, it's not my fault. It's one's parents' attitude that forces one to tell lies. . . .

* * *

III

Giles was not usually insensible to the beauties of nature,
indeed the poetry that he wrote was mainly concerned with
landscape, the seasons, distant prospects of ecclesiastical
architecture or nostalgia for the mountains, but this morning
he had walked to Bablockhythe, pondered beside the river,
walked back, sat on damp grass under Arnold's pine and
hadn't seen a single branch etched against flying skies, hadn't
noticed cerulean blue in the stripling Thames, had ascended
Cumnor without pining for Great Gable and had trodden
heavily on an unseasonable celandine. Blindly he walked, but
with his inward eye gazing intently on scene after remembered
scene . . .

He saw the little smoking room at Wasdale Head, the blind
drawn, the oil lamp on the table, Peter sprawled on the horse-
hair sofa under the glass case which contained the Rock and
Fell Club's mountaineering library. He was here at last, here
and with Peter, and it seemed too wonderful to be true – he'd
never thought his parents would allow him to accept that
marvellous invitation, had thought they'd write back that
mountaineering was dangerous and who was this Mr Gillespie?
But, on the contrary, they'd written to say that it would be
very nice for him and had sent him money for tips and a
pair of climbing boots and had only said that it seemed rather
odd that he had never mentioned this Mr Gillespie.

Peter – for on that first day, at lunch in the pub on the
Great North Road, he'd said that he wasn't going to be treated
as a master any longer and that Giles for heaven's sake must

call him Peter – was studying a map and Giles was writing a postcard to his mother saying that he'd arrived safely and that Wasdale was lovely. Just as he'd written *Nr. Oxford*, Peter looked up and said, 'Yes, I think Great Gable tomorrow. By the way, has God any place in your life, Giles . . . ?'

The scene shifted. They were swinging down the fellside together from their last climb. The beck ran with them and their shadows too, and the short Cumberland turf was quite golden. 'Of course you must tell them,' said Peter. 'There's no need to make a song and dance about it – just tell them quite simply. Tell them you've been changed and then leave it. Their main fear will be that you're out to change them and so, of course, you are, but, as I said the other day, "Christianity's caught, not taught" – that's not mine, by the way. Leave them alone and they'll *get* interested. Then you can ask them just to give God a trial. . . .'

'Yes,' said Giles, 'but it's *telling* them. . . .'

'Well, surely you don't funk that, my dear man. . . .'

Again, the scene shifted. Now he saw the library at Hodson's Pightle. 'Had enough to eat? Then come and sit down and tell us all about it,' said Patricia. 'It was marvellous,' he said. 'Of course we went up the Pillar.' 'That's difficult, isn't it?' said Hugh, remembering scraps of boring conversations at High Table. 'Some ways are,' said Giles. 'But we went up by the Slab and Notch – that's the easiest. Mr Gillespie' – somehow he couldn't say Peter – 'says that the hills were made for something better than gymnastics.' 'What's he like?' asked Patricia, and Giles's heart missed a beat and he said to himself, now . . . I'll tell them now . . . and aloud he said, 'Oh, he's a marvellous fellow.' Then there was a pause and Giles decided to say, I've something to tell you, and then he decided that that sounded as though he'd a confession to make and of course this wasn't a confession. *He's done such a lot for me.* . . . How would that sound? It would break the ice. Go on, say it. . . .

The clock on the mantlepiece ticked cynically. 'Two plain, two purl . . . oh, damn! Thank you for all those postcards,' said Patricia. . . .

And then, dining-room tea on Sunday. August had walked out too, with a hearty friend also from St Mary's. 'Groupers called on you yet?' asked August and Giles nodded and now was the time only his mouth was full. August's hearty friend burst out laughing. 'They called on me when I first came up,' he said, 'and asked after my ideals.' 'What did you say?' asked August. 'I said that at present I'd only one and she was a platinum blonde with slightly protruding teeth. . . .' 'Very funny,' said Giles with unmistakable sarcasm but he must have mumbled for they only laughed again. When they've stopped . . . when they've stopped cackling . . . said Giles to himself, but before he could get his mouth open, 'Playing any rugger?' asked August's hearty friend. . . .

And now it was December, eight months since he had been at Wasdale Head, eight months since Peter had said, 'Of course you must tell them. . . .' and, 'Surely you don't funk that, my dear man. . . .' And he *had* funked it. Time and again he'd funked it, and it was no use trying to pretend to himself that his mouth had been full or that his mother had interrupted. For eight months every morning during the Quiet Time that he kept though he didn't really belong to the Group

✱ ✱ ✱

yet, it had been the first of the things he meant to do during the day to occur to him, and every evening he had found that he had done all the other things – written the letter, changed the conversation, spoken the kind word, given the money . . . yes, all the things except that one thing, the one thing which at this stage really mattered. And until he did it, though he *was* changed, lived such a different life, was so much nicer, so much happier, knew that there's a purpose in life, that it's not all chance, loved everyone, could even get on with August, he'd have to remain outside. Perfect Truth? How could he claim to be changed and then stand up and say that he was afraid to tell his parents?

Sitting on the damp grass under Arnold's tree, Giles asked for Guidance. Not for the first time, the message he received directed him to go straight into the house and say to Patricia or Hugh – which ever he met first – 'By the way, I'm joining the Oxford Group,' and wait for developments. Why not? There was nothing to be afraid of. It was all perfectly simple.

He got to his feet. A little wind from the south blew in his hair. He felt young and strong. What was that poem which his mother had made them all learn because she said it had more sense in it than most hymns? . . . *Not while the light is dim but now from the heart of joy* . . . Heart of joy? Well, his would be that when he'd told them. . . . He set off running down the hill.

The gate of the drive was open. The car was in the yard. Giles went through the kitchen. 'Come on, Master Giles, you aren't 'arf late,' said the stout misnamed Mrs Frisker.

Giles, suppressing an inclination to say, 'Shut up, Frisky,'

✴ ✴ ✴

said, 'Sorry, Mrs Frisker,' and went through into the dining-room. Hugh with cabbage poised on his fork said, 'Can't you ever be in time, Giles?' and Patricia said, 'I thought you'd been run over.' Nicola said, 'Look here, Giles, I do wish you'd leave Griselda's bridle as you find it,' and August said, 'I say, Giles, do *you* know where the small saw's gone?'

Giles said he was sorry he was late and was it likely that at his age he would get run over? He said he hadn't seen the small saw and how often did Nicola clean the bridle?

CHAPTER SIX

August Behaves Fair

I

Elspeth came to dinner in the blue dress that Patricia had hoped for, and during the meal she and August talked about beagling and horses, and Patricia listened and thought that they were made for one another and watched Elspeth and knew that she knew it, and watched August and was afraid that he didn't know. 'A nice girl,' said Hugh when the children had gone off in the car to the cinema, and filling his pipe he said, 'I notice that she's here a lot. Is August attached to her?' Hugh nowadays avoided such words as 'in love'. 'Attached to', he said, and 'has a *penchant* for', and 'devoted'.

Patricia said crossly, 'Heaven knows. He ought to be. She's nice-looking. She's got as many brains as he has. They've everything in common.'

'Things don't always go like that,' said Hugh vaguely, remembering Hulver, and then he remembered how different August was from the young man he'd been, and he added, 'But of course nowadays there's all this frankness.

Everything's discussed. There's no romance. Messy stuff, romance.' This for Hugh was communicative.

Patricia said, 'No. They haven't much excuse for choosing wrongly. Every novel they read contains an awful warning. They know so much more than we did. Such treachery it was bringing one up with those pretty-pretty notions.'

But Hugh didn't continue the conversation. His pipe was filled. With an escapist's sigh, he sat down at his littered table.

Patricia waited for the children. After eating sandwiches Giles and Nicola went to bed. August stayed smoking a last cigarette. Patricia said with elaborate unconcern, 'It's lucky we've got such nice neighbours.'

August said, 'Have we? Who?'

'The Camerons to begin with,' said Patricia. 'I think Elspeth's one of the nicest girls I know.'

'Yes,' agreed August. 'She's quite a satisfactory person.' He flicked ash on the carpet and said, 'Outdoor, but has nice frocks and powders her nose.'

'Nice-looking. And she's got brains, too,' said Patricia.

'And a sense of humour. And she's awfully decent about ninepenny seats and that kind of thing.'

'She's a dear,' summed up Patricia and silence fell.

And there's Gwen, thought August, she's got no brains, she's afraid of dogs, she laughs at the wrong things, and yet it's her I can't keep away from. If I were old, thought August, if I were forty . . . me on one side of the fire and Elspeth on the other . . . we'd have plenty to say . . . but in the meantime there's no thrill in thinking of Elspeth, whereas with Gwen

. . . Oh, hurry up, time, thought August, pitching his cigarette end into the fire and yawning dismally.

Patricia, more or less satisfied, said, 'Surely Nicola must be out of the bath by now. . . .'

II

Patricia always remembers how slowly spring came that year. She had got used to her plate before anything but the meek irritating snowdrops had flowered, and when at last the east wind dropped in the night and the repressed daffodil buds burst into a fanfare of trumpets, her low spirits revived as abruptly. Spring, she reiterated, could mean little to a woman over forty with false bottom teeth and an epicene husband, but August had asked Elspeth to tea in his rooms, Nicola had swapped a blouse for a hat with Mary Cumberledge, and Giles had written a sonnet. Oh, she'd not been wrong that December evening when she'd met despair in Beaumont Street; if you'd children, spring couldn't mock you; though, in your own veins, your blood didn't quicken, though the blackbird, singing after tea, merely made you think of spring-cleaning, in *their* veins it leaped and hammered, in them again as the buds burst and the adorable evenings lengthened, you loved and dreamed. . . .

'Spring's come,' she said to Hugh at breakfast.

'Thank goodness for that,' said Hugh. 'Look at this coal bill!'

'Oh well,' said Patricia not looking. 'Man must light his fires.'

* * *

'I daresay,' said Hugh. 'But he must also pay for them.'

'It's all wrong,' said Patricia. 'The fruits of earth should be free to all.'

'Don't be absurd,' said Hugh.

Patricia thought suddenly of her grandfather. Absurd he'd been, absurd that life at Hulver. *His lordship would like the brougham at eleven. . . . We'll have the ballroom redecorated and give a dance for you. . . . Will you be wearing the pearls or the moonstones, Miss? . . . Dinner is served, my lord. . . .* Odd, how years afterwards one could be so suddenly and intolerably homesick. . . . Dear patient hardworking Hugh. . . .

Hugh said, 'What on earth's all this about?' and passed across a letter.

Patricia took the limp half sheet of cheap blue ruled notepaper. The handwriting was neat, legible and tradesmanly.

She read, *Dear Sir, I should like to see you on an urgent matter re Mr Augustus Lindsay. If convenient will call with Mrs Parker at six-thirty today (Tuesday). If unable to keep appointment, should esteem it a favour if you would give me a ring at the above telephone no. Yours truly, Jas Parker.*

'Oh dear,' said Patricia. 'August must owe him money.'

'Then why didn't he send a bill?' said Hugh irritably.

'Perhaps he has and you've not opened it.'

'Nonsense,' said Hugh. 'I always open everything.'

'It may have fallen behind the hall chest,' suggested Patricia.

'If it's money,' said Hugh, 'why does he want to bring Mrs Parker?'

'To back him up. Or perhaps she just wants a nice ride into the country.'

'It can't be that,' said Hugh. 'August has his faults, but I must say he's always been very considerate about money.'

'Perhaps it's something to do with the car,' said Patricia. 'Perhaps August knocked Mrs Parker down and spoilt her beauty and Jas is bringing her as an exhibit.'

'If August had had an accident we should have heard of it before now,' said Hugh rising. 'Well, I'm off. I shall be back to tea so we needn't waste tuppence telephoning to that fellow. Good heavens, it's half past. Where's the key of the garage? Have you seen my driving gloves and where on earth are my spectacles? . . .'

Patricia saw Hugh off and then she went back to the dining-room. Agnes was clearing the table. Patricia picked up the newspaper, took it into the library and sat down on the window seat in the sunshine.

She read the fashion page. Skirts were to be worn with contrasting jackets. Oh splendid, she'd be able to use the perfectly good coat of her brown and white check tweed with a plain brown skirt that she'd be able to get for twelve and sixpence. . . . Oh, dear, another maniac waylaying girls . . . never mind, it was only in Surrey. *Young Oxford Girl Rescued from Drowning.* . . . Gosh, is it anyone that I know? . . .

She read: *Dark-haired petite twenty-five-year-old hairdresser's assistant, Gwendoline Amy Parker, was rescued last night from the River Isis near Hythe Bridge Street. Stalwart blue-eyed giant PC Bloxham, cycling home, heard a splash, dived in fully dressed and succeeded in bringing the girl to the bank where he applied artificial*

✸ ✸ ✸

respiration. Miss Parker is now in the Radcliffe Infirmary. Interviewed at his tasteful home in Abbatoirs Street, Mr Parker, the well-known and highly respected newsagent, stated, 'It beats me. Gwen like most modern girls was the independent kind, but she had no troubles that I know of. She was fond of walking by the water, she must have missed her footing in the dark.' Late last night Miss Parker was reported to be comfortable.

Jas Parker . . . Gwendoline Parker . . . *I would like to see you on an urgent matter re Mr Augustus Lindsay.* . . . Oh, well, Parker's a common name. Stop it, said Patricia to her shaking knees and she told herself, go and find the letter and you'll see – the address will be Iffley Road or Summertown – you *must* have noticed it if it had been Abbatoirs Street. She went into the dining-room. Agnes was sweeping crumbs from the table, using a dustpan and a stiff carpet brush instead of the proper crumb brush and scoop, and she started guiltily and dropped the dustpan. 'Oh, Agnes,' said Patricia, 'did the Professor leave a letter on the table – a blue one?' 'A letter? No, madam,' said Agnes, standing on the mess of dust and crumbs. Hugh sometimes put letters he wanted to forget on the mantelpiece, so Patricia looked there and in the library and the hall and the wastepaper baskets. It was evident that Hugh had crammed the letter into his pocket.

So there was nothing to do but to wait, alternately panicking and laughing at herself for panicking, recalling the appendicitis that had turned out to be stomach ache, the broken neck that had turned out to be a cast shoe, the disgraceful behaviour that on further enquiry had turned out to

88

* * *

be sucking bulls'-eyes during Musical Appreciation. In the afternoon she remembered that you can't worry when you're doing things out of doors, so she went out, cleaned her chicken houses and sawed an exceedingly tough old oak post into logs for the fire. But as she carried the logs into the house, she panicked again. The car was back. Hugh was at home – Hugh with his Peebles background and his Scots Presbyterian morals. . . .

Hugh was quite jocose about the impending visit.

'You'd better change your clothes,' he said. 'Mr Jas Parker won't expect to find a professor's wife in an overall.'

'By the way, what was his address?' asked Patricia, and a queer prayer, please, God, make it Iffley Road, ascended to heaven.

Hugh said, 'I didn't notice.'

Patricia said, 'Where's the letter?'

Hugh took a bundle of papers from his breast pocket. He looked through them, discovered a picture postcard of the Matterhorn, which he showed to Patricia; discovered a receipt for a bill he thought he hadn't paid and sat beaming at it; discovered an admirable translation from Ronsard by a favourite pupil, which he read aloud, praised line by line, and restored to his pocket. Then he said, 'Let me see – what was I looking for?'

Patricia said, 'For Jas Parker's letter.'

'Oh yes,' said Hugh. 'But it's not here. I must have cast it away somewhere.'

'Oh, God!' said Patricia nerves on edge. 'You're always casting things away somewhere.'

✻ ✻ ✻

'Really,' said Hugh, 'I think that's most unfair. I consider myself to be on the whole a most methodical person.'

'Do you? Well, I don't,' said Patricia.

'You surprise me,' said Hugh. He ate a slice of cherry cake. 'After all, the world won't end because I've cast away a letter.'

'I'll go and change,' said Patricia.

She went to her room. After much argument Spartan Hugh had consented to install central heating in the passages and living rooms, but the bedrooms were unheated and generally Patricia hurried through a skimped, shivering toilet. Today, however, warm air, smelling of grass, drifted in through the open windows and she wandered about choosing a green dress and stockings without holes in them and thought of another spring time, the spring time when she had met a man to whom she could speak her heart out . . . a man . . . Hugh Lindsay . . . actually Hugh. You'll double your joys and halve your sorrows someone – some silly sentimental ass – had said to her, but you didn't; you went to live with a man because he was the one person to whom you could speak your heart out, and the years went by and behind respective walls of flesh he grew and you grew, and then something happened and you realised that you and he had grown into quite different people and you couldn't tell him anything, not that you'd overdrawn your account or that you wanted to keep a donkey or that all the long day you had been worrying yourself sick over something that probably wasn't anything. You didn't resent it. It wasn't his fault. Probably – if men notice that kind of thing – he thought the same of you. And you still went on loving him; it didn't alter that . . . oh, you can be one body, thought Patricia, but you can't be one soul. Soul of my soul babble the poets and damnably they mislead us; and, feeling cold now, cold and alone, she took a drab woollen cardigan from her green chest of drawers painted with posies, and slipped it on over her green dress.

'Why,' asked Hugh, 'do you always hide your frocks under that old brown thing?'

'Because it's like an ice house in here,' said Patricia.

As she spoke, the bell rang. Hugh had gone to the expense of having electric bells installed because everyone else had them and people in their position really couldn't, as Patricia had suggested, 'holler'. Sounds came from the hall – a nervous cough, Agnes putting coat and hat on the chest and asking the name. Then, 'Mr and Mrs Parker,' said Agnes, forsaking her good Oxfordshire accent for mincing tones.

Hugh and Patricia said, 'Oh, good evening.' Mrs Parker said, 'How do you do, Mrs Lindsay. And you, Professor?' and Mr Parker said, 'Good day.'

Mr Parker was short, lean, elderly and ill at ease. His head was bald, his forehead deeply lined. He wore pince-nez. His eyes were small and faded and under sagging lids glanced restlessly here and there. He had a bulbous nose, thin lips with a downward droop, and badly fitting dentures, which he munched. He was dressed in a dark grey suit, black boots, a stiff collar and a dark grey tie passed through a ring of rolled gold.

Mrs Parker was short, middle-aged and stout. She was dressed in a long coat of navy blue trimmed with black fur. Her stockings were grey; her strapped shoes black; her small fat hands were tightly encased in good brown leather gloves, fleece-lined. She wore a heavy black felt hat trimmed with Petersham ribbon. She had dark brown eyes under scanty grey lashes and eyebrows; her face was fat and pale with a spreading nose, a heavy chin and lips as thin as those of her husband. She smelled of violets.

Patricia said, 'Do sit down.'

Mrs Parker sat down and said, 'You'll think it queer us calling on you like this, Mrs Lindsay . . .' but Mr Parker broke in.

'Leave this to me, Bessie. Queer it may be, but we've nothing to apologise for. Did you read your paper this morning?' His darting glance rested upon Hugh.

'I looked at the leading article and the foreign news.' In contrast to Parker's sharp indignant utterance, Hugh's voice seemed vague and slow.

Patricia, who had sat down, rose and collected a box of matches and a silver cigarette box presented to Hugh by colleagues at Glasgow University. She could hear her heart thumping and was afraid that the others would hear it too.

'Then you didn't see that last night my daughter, Gwen, was rescued from the Isis? Threw herself in, she did. Wanted to do away with herself, a fine girl like that. And why?'

'Dear me. Dear me,' said Hugh.

Patricia offered cigarettes to Mrs Parker, who shook her head. Patricia, however, took one, lit it, and stood staring into the fire.

'And why?' said Mr Parker. 'Because she'd been going out with your son, that's what she'd been doing, and he took

✳ ✳ ✳

advantage of the poor girl and got her into trouble – that's why.'

There was a moment's silence. Then, 'You surprise me,' said Hugh.

'It was a surprise for us,' said Mrs Parker, opening her bag with a click and producing a lace-edged handkerchief and a still stronger smell of violets. 'A great surprise. Our Gwen's always been such a good girl. A comfort to her mother, that's what she's been.'

'A girl like that to want to take her life!' said Mr Parker and his breath whistled as he drew it in. 'And all,' he said, 'on account of your son.'

Hugh said, 'Let us keep calm,' and passed his hand through his thick untidy grey hair. 'Briefly,' he said, 'you accuse my son of seducing your daughter. To put it crudely, how do you know that it was he?'

'By this. We found it on the poor girl's dressing-table.' He thrust forward a folded sheet of blue note-paper, which Hugh took. He fumbled for his spectacles, put them on and read aloud.

' "*Dear Mum*" . . . Am I really to read this?' asked Hugh.

'Yes, read it,' said Parker impatiently.

' "*Dear Mum, I am sorry to say that I am in trouble, and the cause of it is Mr Augustus Lindsay, an undergrad of St Mary's College, but I don't wish him no harm so don't you neither and don't give him away only I'd like you to know that it was a real gentleman. I am sorry for this what I am doing but I can't bear the shame. Forgive me, Mum and Dad, your broken-hearted Gwen*" Dear me,' said Hugh. 'Dear me.'

'Ah, you're not the poor girl's father,' said Parker. 'I can see that you don't take it hard.'

Hugh said, 'You misunderstand me. I am taking it exceeingly hard. I sympathise with your feelings; I am deeply shocked; but please keep calm and realise that this is not by any means the first time that such a thing has occurred.' He fell silent, looking vaguely before him. Patricia had a feeling that he was thinking not about August but about that rascal Will Shakespeare or young Lord Byron.

Mrs Parker said, 'It's the first time it's occurred in our family. We've always 'eld our 'eads 'igh.'

Somehow the lack of aspirates touched Patricia. She said gently, 'I expect you have. . . . I'm awfully sorry about your daughter, but we can't do much till we've seen August, can we, Hugh?'

Hugh folded up the sheet of paper. 'No,' he said. 'Until I've seen my son I can't really give an opinion or make a suggestion of any kind.'

'Well,' said Parker, 'I like that, that I do. There's Gwen's letter plain as a pikestaff. Don't you believe us then?'

'I told you,' said Hugh. 'I have every sympathy with your indignation but I can't say any more until I've seen my son.'

'I'm not a liar,' said Parker and Patricia had opened her mouth to say I'm sure you're not, when Mrs Parker intervened.

'Now, Jim, be reasonable. I'm sure it's all very terrible and nobody understands a mother's feelings but there's no need to get vulgar and common and go calling names. Put yourself in the Professor's place for an instant. You wouldn't go no further, not without a word to your son.'

✱ ✱ ✱

'That's all very well,' said Parker, 'but I hired a car to come here.'

'Well,' said Mrs Parker, 'we can afford it. And more.'

Hugh said, 'Look here, Patricia – supposing I ring up the porter's lodge and get a message to August telling him to take a taxi and come out? If I do it now, I'll catch him before he goes into Hall.'

Patricia spent a moment deciding that certainty, however horrible, was better than any more suspense. 'Yes,' she said. 'Do.'

Hugh went out and she followed him. The telephone was in the lobby. In the hall Hugh turned to her and said, 'Good God, Patricia, this is awful. What's that boy done?'

Patricia said, 'I don't know that I believe them. We must wait till August comes.'

'And then,' said Hugh and unconsciously borrowed a phrase of August's, 'he'll lie like stink. They always do.'

Patricia was going to say that August was truthful. Then she remembered how he had lied about taking Elspeth to a dance and she was silent. Hugh went to the telephone.

When he came back he said, 'August's just come into college. I put it pretty strongly. I said he must come at once whatever his engagements were.'

'Oh, Hugh, how could you? He'll think we've had a crash in the car.'

'Not if he's got a guilty conscience,' said Hugh.

'Perhaps he hasn't. I'd sooner believe him than those Parkers.'

'That,' said Hugh, 'is because August has the inestimable

95

advantages of a clear complexion, fair hair and large blue eyes.'

Patricia said, 'Oh, Hugh, how detached you are!'

'No,' said Hugh. 'I'm feeling this horribly. You know how I was brought up. But you can't live in Oxford without realising that everything . . . everything has happened before. . . .'

Patricia said abruptly, 'Oughtn't we to go back in there?'

'You might go in and tell them that August is coming,' said Hugh.

So Patricia went in. The Parkers were sitting silently on either side of the fire.

Patricia said, 'Would you like a drink or anything?'

'Not in this house I wouldn't,' said Parker but prudently added, 'Not until I've got some satisfaction anyway.'

Mrs Parker said, 'Now Jim. . . .' Then she turned to Patricia and exclaimed, 'Wonderful weather for the time of year.'

Patricia said, 'It is, isn't it?'

After a silence Mrs Parker resumed, 'Very quiet out here.'

Patricia said, 'It is, isn't it?' Then she pulled herself together and said, 'I hope your daughter is none the worse for her . . . for being in the river.'

'Well, Mrs Lindsay I can't say that, seeing as how she was half-drowned at the time. But she's picked up wonderful. We saw her today in the Infirmary – lovely and bright they are, those wards. Of course she was upset to see us. "Oh, Mum," she said, "I *have* been a bad wicked girl." Yes, that's what she said. "A bad wicked girl," she said. And I said, "Now then, Gwen, it's no use upsetting yourself. It's the future you must look to. What's done's done." That's what I said, and you heard me, didn't you, Jim?'

'Too soft by half,' said Mr Parker, and added darkly, 'But I don't blame the *girl*.'

'Still,' said Patricia, 'it takes two.'

'That's what I can't seem to get hold of,' said Mrs Parker dabbing her eyes. 'Our Gwen's been brought up nice – lovely I used to dress her; believe me or believe me not, she never wore the same dress two days. And I never let her play about the roads, Mrs Lindsay. "No, Gwen," I said. "You run straight home from school to Mum and then you won't come to no 'arm." And we've a lovely home, Mrs Lindsay. Only a few weeks ago we had Gwen's own bedroom done up for her – white and mauve. White paint and a mauve carpet and curtains and a lovely mauve eiderdown shot with gold. One thing I will say of Mr Parker, he never grudges what he spends on Gwen.'

Patricia said politely, 'I see she's a lucky girl . . . I mean in her home.'

'That she is and whatever can have come over her I don't know.'

'You can take it from me,' said Mr Parker, 'our girl was not to blame.'

'Well,' said Patricia, 'if you'll excuse me a moment I'll shut up the hens.'

She went out. Hugh wasn't in the hall and the sounds that came from the dining-room were made by Agnes, who, when Patricia looked in, asked once again if angels-on-horseback wanted fish knives. 'Yes – no,' said Patricia and back in the hall saw that the front door was ajar – evidently Hugh, a cat on hot bricks like herself, had gone down the drive. She opened the door. It was a lovely evening. Above the brown roof of the stable the sky was green. A blackbird was singing and it wouldn't end in a futile attempt at suicide in what they *would* call 'the Isis'. Oh, what was the matter with people? When, why and where, for what magnificent bribe had they surrendered freedom? Eve, was it you? You, Moses? When did it all begin?

Hugh came through the gate. He said apologetically, 'I just went down the lane.'

Patricia said, 'I wish August would come.'

'Give him time,' said Hugh.

He began to fill a pipe. Patricia said, 'Have you any gaspers on you?' but as usual he hadn't and she went upstairs to fetch some from her room. Up there she heard the sound of a motor engine and looking from the passage window saw a taxi turn into the drive.

She lit a cigarette and went down. August was leaning forward looking at the meter and as the taxi came to a standstill behind the dark cumbersome laudaulette which had brought the Parkers, he flung the door open, leaped out and paid the driver. Then, 'What on earth's happened?' he said, coming forward, looking charming, honest, candid . . . oh, inestimable advantage, thought Patricia, of fair hair, a clear complexion and large blue eyes!

Hugh said, 'Some people called Parker have come here.'

August said, 'Oh, God!'

'I should think it is "Oh, God!"' said Hugh grimly. 'Do you know what they came to say?'

'I've a fair idea,' said August.

✱ ✱ ✱

'Oh, August,' said Patricia. 'It isn't true?'

He looked down at her. He was thinking that after all there was a lot to be said for truth – when you lied you got flustered, tied up in knots, but when truth was out, whatever it was, however awful, you felt quite calm; everything was simple and easy; you knew what to do. But Patricia couldn't tell what he was thinking and she thought him brazen when he answered, 'If they came to say that I've got Gwen into what I'm sure they call "trouble", it's true.'

Hugh said, 'You astound me.'

Patricia said nothing because all she could think of was a phrase she hadn't used for years: oh, August, you naughty boy!

'I astound myself,' said August, and over Patricia's head he gave a fleeting grin. 'Well,' he said, 'What next? Are they still here?'

Hugh said, 'In the library. We'd better go in.'

August held the door open. Mr Parker was standing with his back to the fire.

'Ah,' he said as August shut the door. 'Here's our young gentleman then.'

'Good evening, everybody,' said August.

'Good evening to you,' said Mr Parker. 'Now then.'

August took out his Woolworth cigarette case, tapped one of his Russian cigarettes on it, tried to make his lighter work, gave up and said to Patricia, 'Any matches?' Patricia gave him a box. He lit his cigarette, threw the match into the fire, blew smoke through his nose, looked candidly at Mr Parker and said, 'Well?'

***

'Well,' said Mr Parker. 'What I want to know is – what do you mean to do about my girl?'

Hugh raised his hand. 'One moment, please, and please let us all keep calm. It occurs to me – Mr Parker, are you sure of your facts? I mean girls are apt to get nervous and imagine things, or so I believe. It has happened before.'

'Gwen wouldn't have thrown herself into the river for nothing,' said Mrs Parker. 'She's been brought up nice as I've said once and I'll say again, but she's got her head screwed on the right way.'

'Actually,' said August in a quiet voice, 'Gwen *was* sure. I understand that she saw a doctor before she went and did that silly thing – trying to drown herself, I mean.'

'Silly you call it,' said Parker. 'I like that. And who, may I ask, was to blame?'

Patricia, suddenly exasperated, burst out, 'If you're going to ask questions like that, there's some I want to ask too. One is: why did you let your daughter go about with under-graduates? You must have known that it wasn't a wise thing to do. And here's another: if she was brought up so nice . . . nicely . . . why did she *let* August . . . er . . . get her into trouble? As I said before, it takes two. . . .'

'I daresay,' said Mrs Parker, 'but the girl pays.'

'Well, she must have known that,' said Patricia. 'She's twenty-five – at least so the newspaper said. And according to you, her head's screwed on the right way. If she was silly enough to start an affair with a boy like August, it was up to her to look after herself.'

'Oh, that's how it is, is it?' said Parker. 'Now we know. But just listen here . . .'

Whatever he meant to say was cut short by August. In the same quiet voice he said, 'Really, I can't see the point of arguing. . . . Actually, it's rather embarrassing and anyhow, *I've* something to say. I went to see Gwen this afternoon and, actually, we're engaged.' He fumbled in his pocket. 'On the way back to college I bought an engagement ring.' He opened a blue morocco case and displayed a half-hoop of diamonds. 'Do you think she'll like it?'

Hugh said, 'My God!' Patricia said, 'Oh, August!' Mr Parker munched at his denture and Mrs Parker said, 'My word, it's lovely. Well, this *is* a surprise.'

Hugh said, 'August, have you *any* sense? Do you realise what this means?'

'Yes,' said August flashing his diamonds. 'I shall have to chuck going into the Army and get a job. Actually I'm sick of Oxford.'

'Jobs aren't so easily come by,' said Hugh and added ominously. 'You'll have no degree.' He turned to Parker. 'You realise that August will have no prospects. And I can't afford to keep him.'

Parker rubbed his hands together. His manner had changed.

'Oh, well,' he said, 'I daresay he'll stand as much chance as any other young fellow. University degrees isn't everything. He's had a good schooling, I daresay.'

'It depends on what you call a good schooling,' said Hugh. 'He's been educated for a career, if you understand what I mean. If he merely gets a job – well, then he's been educated in the worst possible way.'

Mrs Parker said, 'I'm only suggesting, but why shouldn't

he continue his studies? Of course, it's not quite as it should be, but after they got married Gwen could come back home for a time and help me.'

'No, thanks,' said August.

Hugh said, 'Well, what do you propose to do?'

'Find a job,' said August, shutting the jewellers' case with a snap and stowing it away. 'Surely,' he said, getting up, 'I can earn my own living. If I can't find anything else, there's a shortage of farm labourers, I believe.'

'Oh, Gwen wouldn't like that,' said Mrs Parker.

'He's only joking, Ma,' said Mr Parker. 'Never you fear. He'll find something as will satisfy Gwen.'

Hugh held forth. 'No one can accuse me of being snobbish – how could I be? My father was a self-made man. I'm a democrat.' He turned to Parker. 'To judge from some things I've heard tonight, I'm more of a democrat, I should imagine, than you are. So you won't take it amiss if I say that, while your daughter would probably be satisfied with three or four pounds a week, August wouldn't be.'

'Well, if I'm not satisfied,' said August, 'I shall have to . . . er . . . work my way up in whatever it is, that's all. I'm not a complete moron. . . .'

Hugh said, 'How many credits did you get in the School Certificate? Two! And I have never been more surprised in my life than when you passed Smalls.'

'But brains aren't everything,' said Mrs Parker. 'When Mr Parker engages an assistant, he looks for character.'

'The less said about August's character the better, I should think,' said Hugh.

✱ ✱ ✱

'Now Professor,' said Mrs Parker, 'you mustn't be too 'ard. Mr Lindsay, or as I suppose I should say, Augustus. . . .'

Patricia said in a strangled voice, 'We call him August. His real name's David. . . .'

'Oh, David's nice,' said Mrs Parker. 'August – that would be after the month, I suppose?'

'No,' said Patricia. 'It was after a very dear horse.'

'A horse?' said Mrs Parker. 'Well, I never did. D'you hear, Jim? Our Gwen was named after her auntie – Gwendoline.'

'Look here,' said August. 'Don't we have to do something intelligent about banns?'

'They have to be called,' said Mrs Parker. 'Oh dear, oh dear, to think of our little Gwen! You'll have to communicate with the clergyman of our parish, Mr Lindsay . . . August . . . David. The Reverend Rodgers. Such a superior man.'

'I see,' said August. 'Well, I'll do that tomorrow. And I'll call at the Radcliffe to see Gwen.'

Mrs Parker got up. 'Well,' she said doubtfully, 'as it's all settled, perhaps there's things Mr Lindsay would like to talk over with his pa and ma. We'd better be going, Jim.'

Parker said, 'Yes, we won't intrude no longer, but there's one thing I will say. I think Mr Augustus Lindsay has behaved very fair. As to what's past, well, of course, that's different, but young people will be young people and it's no use crying over spilt milk, as they say. If all comes to pass as it should do, I hope there won't be no ill will.' He fixed his darting glance on Patricia. 'No ill will on either side.'

'And I hope we'll soon be able to welcome you to our

home,' said Mrs Parker. 'I'm sure you'll find it very nice, Mrs Lindsay. We live well.'

Patricia said, 'Thank you. I hope your daughter will be better soon.'

'You'll be wanting to see her, I expect,' said Mrs Parker. 'I know I shouldn't be able to wait to see my future daughter-in-law. I'm sure you'll love her, Mrs Lindsay. Dark, she is – takes after me. And she speaks lovely – ever so refined.'

August had the door open.

'Where did you leave your coats and things?' he asked. 'In the hall?'

'Well, we'll say good night,' said Mr Parker, munching as he shook hands. Mrs Parker, still wearing her gloves, shook hands too.

August ushered them out and shut the door.

Hugh said, 'My God!'

Patricia said, 'August is stark staring mad.'

Hugh said, 'I don't understand him – that's what cramped my style. Does he want to marry this wretched young woman or is he under the impression that he is doing the right thing?'

Patricia said, 'God knows.'

August came back and stood in the room humming.

Hugh said, 'Look here, August. You've behaved very badly. You've let us all down.'

'I know I have,' said August. 'I'm dreadfully sorry. But it's no use crying over spilt milk and if everything comes to pass as it should do, I hope there won't be no ill will on either side.'

'Oh,' said Patricia nerve-wracked, 'Don't quote that awful man.'

* * *

'He *is* rather a flop,' said August, 'but Gwen can't help her relations. After all,' he said to Hugh, '*your* father was a builder.'

Hugh said, 'Yes. But he was also a man of remarkable character.'

'And I'm sure,' said August, 'that many a bar sinister disfigures Mummy's coat of arms.'

'I suppose,' said Hugh, 'that you are trying to excuse yourself by proving that all this has happened before. You're right. It has. The world is full of fools and always will be. I'm not crying over spilt milk, August. On the subject of your quite deplorable behaviour I shall never say another word. I'm thinking of the future. Do consider what you are tying yourself down to – some job that you may hate . . . an unsuitable wife . . . for two or three times longer than you've lived already . . . forty or fifty years. . . .'

The gong rang.

'I've thought that all out,' said August, 'and I've made up my mind. Actually, I don't consider Gwen unsuitable. There are lots of jobs I'd like outside the Army. And anyhow, ten to one there'll be a war.'

'Oh, August,' said Patricia, 'one doesn't get married thinking of the loopholes. . . .'

'I wasn't,' said August. 'I was only thinking of the time I've wasted on Applied Tactics. That was the gong, wasn't it? Can I stay to dinner? I'm as hungry as hell. . . .'

CHAPTER SEVEN

✱ ✱ ✱

That's Over

I

'What are we to tell the others?' asked Patricia.

Hugh, who had a free morning, followed her down the path and said, 'God knows. Look at the spinach.'

'Coming along nicely,' agreed Patricia. 'We'd better both tell the same story. I've had a postcard from Giles. He's walking out to tea this afternoon.'

'What about telling him the truth?' said Hugh not meaning it but forced as always by his analysis of himself – an upright Scot – to proffer the suggestion.

'Oh, I can't,' said Patricia. 'How can I? And then, there's Nicola.'

'Well,' said Hugh, 'you'd better say quite simply that August's getting married. You can say we haven't met the girl and in case they feel disposed to follow his example, just hint at disapproval. Where are the onions?'

'Yes,' said Patricia. 'I don't see any sign of any onions. Of course you know, Hugh, the girl may be nicer than her

✳ ✳ ✳

parents. Goodness knows I'm not snobbish. I mean, if they'd been farmers or shepherds. . . .'

'I know what you mean – Tess of the D'urbervilles. But I'm afraid this girl won't be like that.'

'No,' said Patricia. 'She speaks lovely and she wouldn't like August to be a farm labourer. Hugh,' she cried, waiting and clutching his arm. 'What will happen to him?'

'I suppose he'll go into a business of some sort,' said Hugh and he looked at her and added, 'You mustn't panic. After all he's not the first young man to make a mess of his life.'

'I know,' said Patricia. 'But he's the first of my children. Do you suppose that Giles is deceiving us too?'

'Not in that way. Giles has always struck me as being rather sexless. But probably he's concealing something. Where are the beans?'

'Oh, I don't know,' said Patricia. 'Anyhow, I can't bear this garden. I thought we were going to be happy here – I *was* happy, and now August has spoiled it all.'

Hugh said, 'Don't be absurd, my dear. August has made a fool of himself but the world won't end – we shall still enjoy beans and onions.'

'I shan't,' said Patricia, and the knot in her throat climbed higher. She slipped her hand from his arm, turned away and fled to the stable, blinded.

She sat down on the cornbin. Hugh wouldn't follow her. When you were 'absurd', he left you alone, saying to himself that it would pass, that you weren't the first woman to cry out her eyes. Once she had cried in a stable and a man had come to her, out of his great house he had come and sat on a

107

cornbin and made life right for her. Oh, what was the use of being clever, knowing so much, seeing so far? It wasn't good wise Hugh that she wanted now but the kind old sinner, her grandfather. . . .

She searched the lips of the dead. There had been tears in his eyes too when Shaun the First had died, but he'd said, 'Don't cry, Pat. Shaun was getting old and stiff and now he's young and strong again and he's hunting wolves in heaven,' and then she hadn't cried. And when a bantam had died, he hadn't said that it was only a bantam, he'd said that lots of people believed in reincarnation and he thought it quite likely that Brownie would be born again in the body of one of Shaun's puppies next spring. What else had he said? He had said that Patricia was no fool and could stand a jar. She dried her eyes.

But this wasn't a jar, she thought then; it was an explosion. House, garden, love, hope, all had gone up in air. She'd worked hard, she'd given up most things to raise this family, to make this home, to be what she was, cheery Mrs Lindsay with a charming house and three nice children, one going into the Army, one not sure yet but perhaps publishing, one still too young to know her own mind but almost certain to do something with horses. Oh, she might as well have given up long ago when she was tired and her back ached and her legs ached in Glasgow! What had been the use of showing August beauty, of teaching him manners, of explaining *noblesse oblige*, of reading *The Idylls of the King* aloud to him, of sending him to Rugby and St Mary's? She might as well have kept her mouth shut, let him push past ladies, gone to lie

✱ ✱ ✱

down on her bed, sent him to a day school and spent the money on her own pleasures. For all his charm, sensibility, ideals, he'd done a hideous thing, and all Hugh could say when your life's work and your life's hope crashed was that August wasn't the first young man . . . Oh, thought Patricia, men don't understand. They get children and that's that. If it was his *Life and Times of Alexander Pope* that had turned out worthless, he wouldn't say that it wasn't the first time and he'd still enjoy onions, but he can't understand that August is *my* work. . . .

She got up, was conscious of the smell of the stable, the adorable monochrome of straw, sacks and rafters. Oh, she'd brought August here; from the soul-destroying smugness of 'Loch Lomond', from the heart-destroying superiority of Merton Street, she'd delivered him and brought him to smell hay, shut gates, walk through mud, 'see no enemy but winter and rough weather'. And it hadn't been any use. When his time came neither this orchard breaking into snow-drifts nor these humble brown roofs, not the love of beasts nor the lift of a hill, no soaring anthem or sun-soaked playing-field, neither a line that you'd rather have written than take a city nor knowing that if you left the gate open you'd have to chase the bullocks had stopped him from behaving like any slum bred lout. . . .

In the yard Agnes was calling, 'Madam . . . the telephone. . . .'

Patricia answered, 'Coming,' and to hide her eyes went round the house and through the french windows of the dining-room.

Giles was speaking. He'd muddled things up. After all, he couldn't come to tea.

'Why not?' snapped Patricia.

He sounded embarrassed. He muttered something about an engagement which had passed from his mind.

Patricia said, 'Frisky's just put a chocolate cake in the oven. I can smell it.'

Giles said wouldn't another day do for the chocolate cake? and Patricia said vulgarly but she felt desperate – wouldn't another day do for the blonde?

Giles laughed and said that it wasn't a blonde but a party of men. Patricia, remembering 'Giles always strikes me as rather sexless', said hastily, feebly, that she hoped they were nice men.

Giles said, 'Mummy, what *is* the matter? You sound like an anxious hen.'

'I'm feeling like one,' said Patricia. 'All right, Giles – some other time. . . .'

II

Later in the day August rang up. He said, 'Is that you? I say, Gwen's out of hospital. Can I bring her to tea tomorrow afternoon?'

Patricia said coldly, 'Very well.'

August said, 'Not if you don't want me to.'

Patricia from force of habit said, 'Don't use a preposition to end a sentence with.' Then she said, 'I do want you to. Giles was coming this afternoon, but now he isn't, so there'll be a chocolate cake. Yes, do.'

August said, 'Right,' and rang off.

Patricia told Hugh. He said, 'Yes, we'd better get it over. And whatever she's like, Patricia, don't despair. Women are so adaptable. . . .'

'That,' said Patricia bitterly, 'is all you know. . . .'

III

Patricia had always loved tea time at Hodson's Pightle.

The dining-room had been simply and spasmodically furnished. There was a round Victorian table inherited by Hugh; at one time she had hated it, christened it Albert and covered it with darned damask cloths which Blanche had given her, but now it was fashionable and her pride. Against one wall stood a deal dresser painted brown, a relic of the days when the room had been the farmhouse kitchen; the children's silver christening mugs hung there and blue plates, mostly riveted, stood on the shelves. The worn carpet was fawn colour; the chairs were green, cane-seated and painted with roses, a set that she had fallen in love with and bought from a North Oxford junk shop; the faded pink-striped brocade curtains had been bought at a country house sale. So there wasn't a colour scheme and there wasn't a period, but Patricia didn't mind that; she had been brought up in rooms where furniture had been accumulating since the battle of Senlac and considered colour schemes and period furnishing only suitable in hotels.

Tea was to be in the dining-room as usual and Patricia, waiting for August and Gwen, sat in the library with Hugh. Since she had received the Parkers in her green dress, she no longer liked it, so she hadn't changed, but was wearing a tweed skirt, a short-sleeved shirt and a horsey tie. She had been out in the rain and her naturally curly hair had wound itself into wild corkscrews. She looked like a harassed girl.

Hugh didn't speak. For once in his life he was reading one of the erudite monthlies to which he subscribed.

There were voices in the hall. Somebody – obviously not one of the family – was wiping shoes on the mat . . . wiping them meticulously . . . still wiping them. Then the library door opened and August's voice, level and strained, said, 'Well, here we are,' and Gwen Parker came tripping in.

Patricia got up, went forward, said, 'How do you do?' and was conscious of a plump hand in an embroidered black kid glove.

'Very well, thank you, Mrs Lindsay,' said Gwen.

Then Hugh shook hands and Patricia looked at Gwen. She was short and plump and she looked like a pouter pigeon because she wore a white blouse with a frill over her well-developed bosom and had hard slim hips and strutted on her high-heeled patent leather shoes. She had a soft round face, a high colour, big brown eyes, which bulged slightly, a tip-tilted nose, a small mouth and her mother's heavy chin. She wore pearl beads, a black coat and skirt, the white blouse, the black and white gloves, gossamer stockings of flesh colour and the shiny shoes. On her dark smooth head was perched a hard little hat adorned in the latest fashion with a tiny white bird.

'Do sit down,' said Patricia.

Gwen sat down. August said, looking at his shoes, 'It was awfully muddy coming here.'

'Did you come by the ferry?' said Hugh.

'Yes,' said August.

Patricia said, 'Have you been here before?'

'No, Mrs Lindsay,' said Gwen. 'I don't care for walking.' She giggled and added, 'I like to ride.'

'Oh, do you?' said Patricia. 'That's splendid. We've got an old hunter . . .'

'Oh, I didn't mean on horseback, Mrs Lindsay. I can't bear horses. I meant in a car.'

'Oh, I see,' said Patricia. 'Why didn't we think of it, Hugh – we ought to have fetched her.'

'Oh, that's quite all right, Mrs Lindsay. We bussed it to the footpath so it wasn't so far. I must say I don't care for the Oxford buses. Mum and I are always on at Dad to buy a car.'

Patricia said, 'I think one gets awfully tired of motoring.'

Gwen said, 'I'd like the chance.'

August got out of his chair.

'What about tea?' he said. 'Are they in or shall I do something?'

'Frisky's in,' said Patricia, 'but you might go and look like tea.'

August pitched a half-smoked cigarette into the fire and went away. He didn't look unhappy, Patricia thought, but his always rather inexpressive face had lost something. He smiled, met your eyes, was at ease, but he looked controlled.

Hugh was no use at all. Patricia said, 'The rain has spoilt all my poor daffodils.'

Gwen said, 'I suppose it's what we must expect. I don't care for this time of year. I like the winter. You can draw the curtains then and be cosy and enjoy yourself with a box of chocs and the wireless going, in front of a nice warm fire.'

Patricia said and could have kicked herself, but, sitting beside this cocksure little creature you didn't care for so much, how could you remember the desperate thing she'd done? 'But you can't bathe.'

Gwen said, 'I don't care for the water. I can't swim. Last year at Bognor . . .'

August, putting his head round the door, said, 'Tea.'

Patricia led the way. Gwen sat down and peeled off her gloves, disclosing scarlet nails, cut to points, and August's diamond ring.

'Have you seen this, Mrs Lindsay?'

'Er . . . yes,' said Patricia. 'I hope you like it.'

Gwen smiled archly at August and said, 'I should say I do.'

'Bread and butter?' said August. 'Jam?'

There was bread and butter and a fruit cake and the chocolate cake, of which Patricia said reassuringly, 'Home-made.'

'Mum always gets our cakes from Odell and Grimshawe's,' said Gwen. 'Iced cakes. They're lovely. I expect we shall get the wedding cake there.'

Patricia didn't want to talk about the wedding. There was always a hope . . . hope of what? Well, perhaps they'd quarrel . . . they *must* quarrel, August, who loved Griselda and beagling and rain in his face, and Gwen, who couldn't bear horses and didn't care for water but liked chocs and the wireless going and riding in a car. Oh, God, make them quarrel. . . . 'More tea?'

✳ ✳ ✳

'Pardon?' said Gwen.

Hugh was studying his tea spoon. August said, 'More tea, Gwen?'

'No, thank you, Mrs Lindsay. I've had sufficient.' Gwen opened her shiny black bag, took out a lace-edged handkerchief and wiped her lips.

'Well,' said Patricia, 'let's adjourn then.'

August took a handful of lumps from the sugar basin. 'I'm going to see Griselda.'

'Would you like to go and be introduced?' Patricia asked Gwen.

She shook her head and the little bird shook too. 'That's the horse, isn't it? No, thank you, Mrs Lindsay. I'd be ever so scared. I expect it's muddy too, out in the fields.'

Patricia led the way back into the library. Hugh disappeared.

Patricia produced cigarettes. Gwen chose a turk and smoked it daintily.

'Mum says I oughtn't to smoke now, but I tell her that's old-fashioned. The doctor didn't mention it. He told me to eat what I fancied and not get overtired.'

'I suppose you've left your work?'

'Oh yes, Mrs Lindsay. All that standing would have been too much for me, besides, after the crazy way I acted, I shouldn't have liked to go back there. Still, let bygones be bygones. I'm busy over my trousseau now.'

'I expect you are.'

'I'm making all my undies – a lovely pinky peach. I'm ever so fond of sewing, Mrs Lindsay. I've got one pair of cami-knicks finished already, embroidery and all. Mum's started on the nighties. I think they're ever so much better style than pyjamas, Mrs Lindsay, don't you?'

'Well actually, I always wear pyjamas,' said Patricia. 'But perhaps I'm old-fashioned.'

'I shouldn't call them old-fashioned, Mrs Lindsay. I think they're rather actressy, that's all. You see, I'm not one to follow that class of person. I go for style.'

Patricia made an approving noise.

'I'm not film-struck, either, Mrs Lindsay. You mustn't think I'm that kind of girl. Of course I like to go to the pictures now and then. I'm not a killjoy. But my ideel is to have a dear little home of my own and keep it ever so nice. I'm that kind of girl.'

'I see.'

'I'll make David a good wife, Mrs Lindsay, never you fear.'

But August didn't want a good wife or a dear little home kept ever so nice. You didn't when you were twenty-one and had meant to go into the Army and go to India and wear a scarlet mess jacket and dance at Simla and play polo . . . Oh, if he had had to get into a mess with a girl, why couldn't the girl have been Elspeth, who talked the same language, loved Griselda and beagling and rain in her face? . . . But Elspeth wouldn't have got into a mess with August – she'd have told him to go to hell with his improper suggestions . . . oh, August, how could you, and with a girl like this . . . oh, August, how far you've gone from me. . . .

'I'm sure you will,' said Patricia, 'only I do feel that you're both rather young to want to settle down.'

★ ★ ★

'Oh, but Mrs Lindsay,' cried Gwen aghast at her ignorance. 'Young marriages are all the thing now – look at the smart set! And I made sure you'd be ever so pleased that David had given up the idea of going into the Army – fancy him going to India, all that long way away from you! And in those parts, Dad says, there's always fighting.'

Patricia said, 'Well, you see, the men of my family have always been soldiers,' and as she spoke August opened the door. He must have heard her but he came forward smiling, saying that Gwen had been right, the paddock was a sea of mud, and Griselda hadn't been a bit grateful for eight lumps of sugar but had slobbered all over him looking for more. 'Oh, how nasty,' said Gwen, and August looked down at her affectionately and said they'd better be going or he'd be late for Hall.

Gwen got up, smoothed the creases from her skirt and drew on her gloves, easing on each finger separately, not dragging them on as Patricia did and everyone else she knew. 'Ready?' said August and Gwen said, 'Goodbye, Mrs Lindsay. Pleased to have met you and you must pay us a visit soon and see all my things.' 'What things?' asked August. 'Never you mind, Mr Nosey,' said Gwen archly. 'He wants to know too much, Mrs Lindsay, doesn't he?'

Patricia said, 'Where's your father, August?'

August went to the door and called out, 'We're going,' and Hugh came in saying, 'What, already?' He wore his dazed yanked-back look and Patricia felt a sudden surge of resentment. This afternoon for the first time he had met the girl whom his son was to marry, and she was vain, brainless,

117

common, a chatterbox, all that he deplored, but he wasn't heartbroken: while she'd sat in the library listening to the chatter she'd wanted to scream, cry, hit the girl on the head with the poker, but he had been able to tell himself that he wasn't the first man to dislike his daughter-in-law and with his escapist's sigh had sat down to comment on some commentary, to criticise some criticism, to pile words on words. . . .

'Goodbye,' said Hugh blinking. 'August, you must let us know your plans.'

August was helping Gwen into a shiny black raincoat strapped and faced with white. He handed her a smart black umbrella, which she slung round her wrist with a silk cord. 'I will,' he said, as he struggled into his dilapidated burberry and, standing aside to let Gwen pass out first, he turned his head and smiled at Patricia. Was it a pleased smile, a proud smile, or was it rueful, was it desperate? . . . There had been a Crispin who had laughed aloud on the scaffold and August was a Crispin through and through. . . .

IV

'Well,' said Hugh, 'that's over.'

'Is it?' said Patricia. 'Or is it just begun?'

'I don't know what you thought,' said Hugh timidly, 'but considering her parents she didn't seem to me such a bad child after all. I mean she's not one of those ultra-modern young females and August will soon break her of saying pardon and wearing a new mackintosh and that kind of thing.

After all, that kind of thing's only superficial. Her heart's in the right place, I should say.'

'Her heart,' said Patricia, 'is in a dear little home that she's going to keep ever so nice, Mrs Lindsay, and in a trousseau of lovely pink-peach cami-knickers, of which she has already finished one pair. There she sits,' said Patricia growing hysterical, 'inexorably stitching cami-knicks and nothing, nobody, not even God can stop her, and, as you say so smugly, she's not one of those ultra-modern young females – whatever August thinks or feels or suffers, she'll never let him go.'

'August has made his bed and he must lie on it,' said Scottish Hugh.

V

Strutting down the drive Gwen said, 'Well, that's over and done with. I daresay many girls in my position would have acted awkward but I was just my natural self, I chattered away to your mother and I could see that towards the end she quite took to me. You couldn't expect much at first – I mean you can't blame her if she was ready for a real fast little piece of goods to come marching in. But as soon as I was left alone with her I made her understand that I wasn't that kind of girl.'

'How did you manage it?'

'Oh, I just told her my ideel – to have a dear little home of my own . . . so it is, David.' She slipped her arm through his. 'I'll keep it ever so posh for you, dear, so that you'll just love coming home.'

$\ast$ $\ast$ $\ast$

'Gwen,' said August, 'you've been reading advertisements. One doesn't really come home because the curtains have washed without shrinking or because there's somebody or another's shrimp paste for tea.'

She pressed his arm.

'Well, that's not the only reason, of course, but it must make a difference. I mean, to come back to a nice bright home. Your place . . . well, I mean it's big – bigger than *I* should want – but it's only a sort of farmhouse, isn't it? and I must say I do think those maids let your mother down. The lounge mantelpiece was *thick* dust and if I kept a cook I'd see that she iced the cake when I had company. . . .'

They had reached the end of the lane. Griselda, who had trotted down the paddock on the other side of the hedge, was standing at the gate to see the last of them; her head was thrown up and the light south-west wind was blowing her mane. August gently removed the black kid glove that lay slug-like on his arm and walked to the gate. His shoes squelched in the mud; he smelled wet grass, wet horse; he saw over the orchard hedge and the apple branches the brown roof stained with yellow lichen of Hodson's Pightle. 'Goodbye, Griselda,' he said and his heart, that had been lead for days so that nothing hurt it, melted suddenly, for this was goodbye to everything, to the life he'd lived and the life he'd meant to live, to horses and mud, to hedges and grasslands, to houses that were only sort of farmhouses, to libraries that had dust on the mantelpiece, to his own language, to his own people. August, you must let us know your plans. . . . A hundred times he might revisit Hodson's Pightle but never again would be of it, never again would he be one of the children. . . . Already he knew that Gwen with her soft round face and plump small hands was his tyrant; she wouldn't bully him but with 'Fancy!' and 'I should have thought . . .' she'd take his soul from him; she'd get her villa and her iced cakes and her suites of furniture, and with somebody's shrimp paste and somebody else's soap flakes, with honeymoon hands and tropical lips, by remembering that he'd seduced her and that she'd thrown herself into the river for love of him, she'd hold him till he forgot the smell of grass and the smell of horses, till he began to think that after all there was something in amenities, something in keeping dry and being safe, till he began to wonder what on earth fellows wanted to risk their necks for, what pleasure there was in having mud on your shoes and rain in your face.

The brisk voice of the angel with the flaming sword spoke to him, saying, 'Come along now, dear. You can't stand talking to that old horse all night. . . .'

CHAPTER EIGHT

We've Lost Them

Giles said, 'I say, Mummy, what's all this about August getting wed?'

'Well,' said Patricia, 'it's as I told you. He's marrying this Parker girl. I think it's very unwise myself. He's much too young and he's spoiling all his chances. But he's twenty-one and legally he can do as he likes, so we can only make the best of it.'

Giles, holding the basket while she piled the guinea fowls' eggs into it, said, 'She tried to commit suicide, I gather.'

'Yes,' said Patricia, 'but I don't want to talk about it.'

Giles, however, did. All his life, quite subconsciously, he had been jealous of August, jealous because August was the elder, the stronger, could run faster, climb higher, swear worse, hadn't spots, hadn't fears, was always obliging and sweet-tempered and possessed, by the mere chance of primogeniture, that place which – so Giles had read somewhere – is without will or reason reserved in every woman's heart for her eldest son. Subconscious jealousy, unable to force an outlet through a nature passionately in love with virtue, twisted, grew, expressed itself in pity – poor old August, how much he misses. . . . August's the sportin' member of the family. . . . We pass it off with a laugh but August's definitely hearty. . . . I can just see you as a retired Colonel, August. . . . Though Giles would have been horrified to realise it, the rumour that August was making an ass of himself over a town girl, the news that his sin had found him out had not displeased him and – still quite subconsciously – he was longing to hear his mother say, we're furious with August, and, we shall never feel the same about August again. If she had said anything like that, Giles, remembering much tolerance, innumerable small kindnesses, farther back, which among the three of them had never bagged or fained, would have been up in arms for August; as it was, when Patricia said that she didn't want to talk about it, he knew that he did and mistook his motive, thinking how insanely difficult it's going to be with a skeleton in the cupboard; how perfectly simple it could be if we were all frank about it.

'Oh, Mummy,' he said, 'how pre-war, of you!'

Patricia was stung. She remembered Blanche and her not mentioning. She said, 'It's all very well, Giles, but that part of it is August's business.'

Giles, sensitive and fastidious, couldn't bear to be told to mind his own business. He hadn't been prying – only wanting to share. He said so. Following his mother through the orchard he said, 'I think that's rather unfair. I was simply trying to avoid skeletons. Rumour has it that the Parker tried to drown herself because she was going to have a baby. It sounds incredibly *East Lynne* but it seems to be true and it's no

* * *

use being ostriches. I mean, if we're all perfectly frank, it'll be so much simpler.'

'Will it?'

'Oh, yes. I've learned that lately.' And now, at last, without the least difficulty or embarrassment, just – he supposed afterwards – because all those other times he had tried to walk before he could crawl, hadn't been ready, he was able to tell her, 'Perfect truth . . . why not? . . . it makes everything so absolutely simple. I've learned that since I've been changed – it's wonderful.'

Patricia, having a job with the warped orchard gate, said absently, 'Why are you talking like a tract, Giles? It's very unlike you.'

'Oh, but I'm not,' cried Giles. 'Honestly, Mummy, there's nothing tractish about it. It's just the only sane way of living. It's going to alter everything.'

'*Giles!*' said Patricia.

'Yes?' said Giles eagerly.

'You don't mean to say that you've joined the Groupers*?'

* The Oxford Group was founded in the 1920s by Frank Buchman, an American Christian evangelist, and was aimed at transforming individuals – and ultimately the world – by setting absolute standards of honesty, purity, unselfishness and love. It held 'houseparties' and larger meetings at which members were encouraged to confess sins and surrender to divine guidance. For several years it held an annual 'houseparty' in Oxford: attendance in 1930 was 700, but by 1935 it had risen to 10,000. In 1938 the Group changed its name to Moral Rearmament.

* * *

'Yes, I have,' said Giles, his face lit up and his hazel eyes dancing – like a kid at Christmas, she thought, like a girl at her first party. 'It's marvellous, Mummy. You don't know what a difference it's made to me.'

'Oh, Giles, you *are* an ass,' said Patricia.

Giles looked down at her. It was pathetic . . . a woman of her age . . . a world-wide revolution . . . and that inadequate private-schoolish phrase. Poor Mummy, inhibited as an adolescent . . . still, Christianity's caught, not taught. He laughed gaily.

'You'll accuse me of "being pi" next. I can see it coming. After all, is it so dreadful – I mean, *you* go to church sometimes.'

Patricia said, 'Shut the gate. Going to church is one thing and foaming at the mouth is another.'

'But we don't foam at the mouth,' said Giles, laughing. 'Darling, it's simply that you keep God in the wardrobe with your Sunday clothes but He's with us all the time.'

There wasn't an answer to that. Long ago when he had thought it worth while to argue, Hugh had proved to her that her religion was indefensible. She believed that God had made the world and counted His sparrows. She believed that He controlled the weather, prospered the harvest. In fact, as Hugh in exasperation had remarked, her faith was summed up in hymn number 573. It was such a childish faith, he had told her: if it had been reasoned, serious, he wouldn't have minded; and Patricia had seen that it was absurd and had always been surprised at the end of a long and learned disquisition to find it quite unshaken. Yet Giles was right.

Firm though her faith was, she didn't pray regularly; as a girl after a good gallop she had thanked God for His mercies, as a woman she had petitioned Him passionately whenever any of her children had a temperature over ninety-nine. She didn't want to start an argument that she knew she'd get the worst of, so she said, 'You can have that without joining anything.'

'You can't share if you've no one to share with,' said Giles. 'Besides, what would be the use of one person? I mean, this is world-wide . . . it's a revolution.'

'Nonsense,' said Patricia.

Hugh was on the terrace. He said, 'It appears to be tea time.'

Patricia said, 'Sorry, I didn't hear the bell. I was collecting gleenies' eggs – look at them! And Giles has been telling me that he's joined the Group. Isn't it idiotic?'

Giles said, 'Mummy disapproves. It's odd – I mean to disapprove of my being happier. . . .'

'But you've always been happy, haven't you?' said Patricia.

'No, I haven't,' said Giles. 'Before I was changed I was definitely repressed and miserable.'

'Oh, Giles,' said Patricia, the ground slipping away beneath her feet as she thought of their summers, their Christmases; Rugby; Hodson's Pightle; Griselda; the books she'd given him; his room she'd made so nice for him. 'Oh, Giles,' she said again and was dismally silent.

'Well, Giles,' said his father, 'this is very foolish of you. You must have known we wouldn't like it. You've heard my opinion of the Group.'

★ ★ ★

'I have,' said Giles, 'but won't you wait and see? I can't expect you to take my word for it now, but you'll see presently how much happier and better I am in every way. Then perhaps you'll feel inclined to give God a trial yourselves. . . .'

'Oh, shut up Giles,' said Patricia.

Giles swallowed back some retort, smiled at his mother and said, 'Well, where shall I put these eggs?'

'Give them to Frisky.'

Giles went indoors and Hugh said, 'Well, let's have tea.'

'Oh, Hugh,' said Patricia, 'I never thought it of Giles.'

'My dear,' said Hugh, 'don't worry. It's only a phase. I suppose that in my time it was Doubts.'

'That wasn't a phase,' said Patricia, sitting at the table. 'It lasted with you.'

'But not with all of us. Don't distress yourself. I know young men.'

'But this isn't young men,' said Patricia and her voice broke as she said, 'It's my Giles.'

Hugh shrugged his shoulders as Giles came in.

Giles said, 'Mrs Frisker was busy so I put the eggs away.'

'Today's good deed,' said Patricia. 'Or am I thinking of the Boy Scouts?'

'You are thinking of the Boys Scouts,' said Giles amiably.

Hugh frowned at her and when Giles had gone he told her: 'You know it's no use making fun of him. That won't do any good at all. Much better to accept the fact and let him get it out of his system.'

Patricia made no answer. She went to fetch in Griselda under rosy clouds and budding apple branches, remembering how pleased the boys had been that first spring when they'd seen the orchard in blossom. But those good days were over now, she thought; they'd outgrown all that, and they'd out-grown her and anything that she could do for them. Oh, she wasn't possessive. She'd wanted them to think for themselves; she'd never tried to force her opinions on them; always she had said, it doesn't matter which I like best: take the one that appeals to you. But that hadn't worked. August, a Crispin she would have said, an open-air man, a lover of horses, had kicked the mud off his shoes and was gone to a villa life with the last girl in the world she would have chosen for him; Giles, the charming dreamer, whom she had thought so content among these hills and meadows, beside this river, had, all the time, been 'definitely repressed and miserable'. Oh, God, thought Patricia, her heart like lead, what more could I have done for them? and she thought of the girl she had been and the woman – the so different woman – that their needs had made of her. They've sucked me dry and left me, she thought, calling coop to Griselda, and she remembered how pleased they'd been with Griselda once, yet now they had their girls and their Groups they no longer cared for her. 'Old lady, we've lost them,' she said. 'We've lost them – all but Nicola,' and then she remembered the old saying that your son is your son till he gets him a wife but your daughter's your daughter all her life. Perhaps it's true, she thought, and remembered times when, talking about clothes or insides or how tiresome boys were, she'd felt a different, less fervent but more comforting, perhaps deeper love for Nicola. Men, she reflected, leading Griselda by a lock of her mane towards the stable, aren't fundamentally

* * *

faithful; silly idealists, they are, chasing will-o'-the-wisps, running round in circles, crying after impossible things like God and Beauty. Johnny-head-in-airs they are, she thought, flibberty-jibbets agog for new loves, new worlds; but Nicola's got a steadfast heart, she thought, seeing the smooth brown head, the grave brown face, the look of a woodland creature, silent and withdrawn. . . .

Griselda plodded into the stable. Patricia fetched pale cool oats, dark green, light green and golden chaff and pinkish geometrical bran. Once upon a time the children had quarrelled over who should feed Griselda. Where were they now? . . .

CHAPTER NINE

✱ ✱ ✱

A Marriage Has Been Arranged

I

Hugh said that it was no use being hole-and-cornery and insisted on announcing in *The Times* that a marriage had been arranged and would take place very quietly on April the twenty-ninth between Augustus David, elder son of Professor and Mrs Lindsay of Hodson's Pightle, Ferry Hinksey, and Gwendoline Amy, only daughter of Mr and Mrs James Parker of Oxford. Colonel Cameron, glancing through the paper at breakfast, said, 'My God.'

Elspeth was used to that. She grinned at her mother, went on tapping the incredible shell of one of the guinea-fowl's eggs, which Giles Lindsay had brought on his way back to Oxford the previous evening, and wishing that Giles hadn't been in such a tearing hurry that she hadn't had time to ask him quite casually what August was doing these days.

'What's happened, Frank?' asked Celia Cameron.

Elspeth said, 'Another injustice to Scotland?'

The Colonel said, 'No, no,' and rustled the paper. Then he

said, 'Your young friend August Lindsay's engaged to be married.'

'Engaged?' echoed Celia.

The Colonel didn't answer. Still under cover, he remarked, 'A lot of damned nonsense being talked in the House of Commons.'

Though her egg was cracked now, Elspeth went on tapping it. Her heart had missed a beat; she felt sick; her knees trembled. August engaged, he'd said. . . . August engaged to be married. . . . It couldn't be true. . . . Life wasn't like that. . . . Life had always been lovely. . . .

Her voice was quite firm as she said, 'Who's August engaged to?'

The Colonel didn't need to turn a page. He said, 'Girl called Parker. Gwendoline Amy, daughter of Mr and Mrs Parker of Oxford. Ever heard of them?'

'No,' said Elspeth.

'Nor have I,' said Celia. 'It's very odd. Giles came last night with these eggs but he didn't say a word about it.'

'What's Lindsay thinking of?' asked the Colonel. 'I thought that boy was going into the Army. No regiment will take a married subaltern – surely even dons know that?'

'Patricia would, if he didn't,' said Celia, wishing that she were cleverer, a great deal cleverer, clever enough to know a broken heart from a sore one. 'Anyhow,' she said, only able to see a corn-coloured lock and a round brown cheek, and feeling tigerish, 'Who is this girl?'

'Don't ask *me*,' said her husband. 'People do such damned odd things these days.' So they do, he thought. Fifty years ago, when men were men, it would have been plain sailing, a clear case for a horsewhip. . . . But nowadays with all this friendship . . . damn it, he thought, there are no rules to go by.

Elspeth, eating her egg and hating it, said, 'Why's it so odd? I mean, why shouldn't August get engaged if he wants to?'

Good girl, thought the Colonel and snapped out, 'Too young. Spoiling all his chances.'

'It seems odd,' said Celia plaintively, 'because we've heard nothing about it. I mean, considering what friends we are. It's not like dear Patricia to be so stealthy.'

'Perhaps she's not too pleased,' said the Colonel. 'Got a lot of sense, that woman.'

Elspeth said, 'Well, I'm going to feed my horse,' and Celia said, 'No toast or anything, Elspeth?' Elspeth said, 'No, thanks. Keeping my weight down,' and shot out through the hall into the shining April morning. Like Patricia, who'd wanted her for a daughter, she took her trouble to the stable and, filling buckets, changing rugs, wondered what life was going to be like without that light over it; if you could go back to being what you'd been before you got that answer; why, since your heart was only a muscle, it should ache so damnably. Oh, she didn't blame August. He'd given her presents – a sandwich case, a safety pin with a fox's mask on it, a yellow silk handkerchief depicting a steeplechase from the Burlington Arcade – he had danced half the night with her, gone out of his way in snow storms to ride home with her, but he had never said anything. . . . It was her own fault; she'd been a silly sentimental Edwardian ass to think that way of him. On his

side it had just been friendship . . . after all, she wasn't pretty.
. . . She could see the girl he'd fallen for, a lovely slinky plucked
and varnished blonde. That was the kind of girl men loved
nowadays; it wasn't any use being honest, unselfish, truthful,
loyal or brave. Never mind, there were still horses – yes, still
horses, Blackbird – and when summer was through with its
saccharine roses and its soppy nightingales, there would still
be plough and grassland, and a south-west wind in your face,
and the sound of the horn in the wood, and the sudden heart-
lifting crash of hound music. . . .

Elspeth set down the bucket with a clatter, swallowed a
lump in her throat and blew her nose. Damn it, she wasn't the
first girl to take a toss and get up and mount and ride on
again. She picked up a pitchfork, smiled at the hearty pukka-
sahib-ish metaphor but found it comforting. . . .

II

Gwen, coming down late in a mauve dressing gown trimmed
with swansdown, said, 'Mum – is it in?'

'Yes, duck,' said Mrs Parker, who was clearing away her
husband's breakfast. 'Dad brought the paper in from the
shop. There it is. He left it for you.'

Gwen picked up *The Times*, which was lying on the fumed
oak sideboard and rustled through the unfamiliar pages.
'Ah,' she said, 'here it is. Looks lovely, doesn't it? But why do
they say "very quietly"?'

'Goodness knows,' said Mrs Parker, adjusting the fit of
her brightly patterned overall. 'Unless,' she burst out, 'it's

because they don't want to ask their posh friends – think it won't be good enough.'

'David says they haven't got any posh friends. He said so the other day when I said, "I wonder what your posh friends will think of me".'

'That's as it may be. All I know is that he's got some ladyship or other for his auntie.'

'That's his Aunt Angela. Lady Langdale. But they've got no money. David said they wouldn't be able to afford to come from the Riviera.'

'Well,' said Mrs Parker, 'that sounds funny to me. Titled people, too. *I* shouldn't like to own that I couldn't afford a railway ticket.'

'I must say I should have tried to think up a better-sounding excuse,' said Gwen, folding *The Times* and replacing it on the sideboard. 'My, that's a dry paper. What's for breakfast, Mum?'

'I've done you a nice bloater. Just a minute, duck. . . .'

Gwen sat with her firm chin cupped in her little hand and dreamed. Supposing David's uncle were killed in a car crash and Lady Angela too, and her son, would David come in for anything? If so, what would David be – Lord Lindsay . . . Lord Augustus Lindsay . . .?

'Here you are,' said Mrs Parker, setting before her daughter a perfectly cooked bloater.

'Mum,' said Gwen, 'I do wish you wouldn't get these plates from Woolys – anybody can see at a glance how much you paid. Whyever can't we have a proper breakfast service . . . modern . . . cream with a nice green line? . . .'

III

Hugh opened *The Times* and said, 'Well, the announcement's in,' and folded back the pages and handed the paper to Patricia; seeing it in cold print, he thought, might help her to realise that deplorable though this marriage was, it was inevitable, must be accepted, made the best of . . . Odd, he thought, tiresome, that in some ways she had never grown up, was still surprised and hurt to find love doesn't last, friends turn traitor, teeth fall out, paint cracks and summer goes. . . .

'I don't want to see the beastly thing,' said Patricia.

Hugh sighed. 'My dear,' he said, 'you really must cultivate a philosophy.'

'I'm not a don,' said Patricia.

'No,' agreed Hugh, 'but you've got to live. It's much easier if you've got a good working philosophy. After all, August wants this young woman.'

'I wish I were sure of that,' said Patricia.

'I've asked him more than once,' said Hugh. 'I spoke to him again yesterday before I posted the announcement. I can tell you he was furious because I indicated that even now one might endeavour to find some other way out. . . . Yes, he really was positively rude to me.'

'I'm sorry,' said Patricia. 'I know you've done everything you could, but really what with him and Giles too. . . . Oh, by the way, I've had a letter from Mrs Parker suggesting that Nicola should be a bridesmaid in mauve shot with gold.'

'Well, as far as I'm concerned she can be. It'll be out of term,' said Hugh.

So when she had seen Hugh off, Patricia wrote to Nicola and asked if she would like to be a bridesmaid, and Nicola wrote back and said that she didn't believe in mumbo-jumbo but would oblige. A few days later she came home, objected to the full and frilly dress and asked many inconvenient questions, which Patricia wearily parried, only to discover later that they had been answered with Perfect Truth by Giles. August went up to London, stayed with friends of his own and went job-hunting; he came back to Hodson's Pightle on the eve of his wedding looking tired, saying it was only the pavements, saying no, he wasn't actually fixed up yet but there were all sorts of things in the offing. It was a trying evening. Nicola, grumbling about wearing mauve frills, sat on the library floor unpacking wedding presents. There was a hunting crop from Elspeth and Nicola cracked it and made hunting noises and Patricia, looking at August, saw his unexpressive face quiver before he got out, 'Idiotic present for a business man. I'll sell it to you, Nicola.' And Giles was being perfectly frank. 'You know, before I was changed I was quite unbelievably snobbish. I should actually have felt awkward about saying that your future in-laws lived in Abbatoirs Street, but this morning I met Mrs Cameron and she asked me where they lived and I told her quite simply and naturally.'

'Don't be silly, Giles,' said Patricia. 'You never were snobbish. We lived in a pink villa ourselves once. None of us have any reason to be snobbish.'

'Oh, but I was,' said Giles. 'Intellectually, too. I used to be proud of myself because I was better at schoolwork than August. . . .'

* * *

'Oh, look August, here's a heavenly shooting stick "with all our love from Uncle Victor and Aunt Angela". Will you sell that, too?' asked Nicola. . . .

CHAPTER TEN

✱ ✱ ✱

Wedding Guests

'Bride or Bridegroom?' whispered young Stanley Higgins.

'Bridegroom – please,' said Patricia.

So that's her, is it? thought Stanley. Nobleman's daughter she may be, but she isn't nearly as smart as our Aunt Bessie. He was doing well in the drapery trade and as he ushered Patricia into a pew he priced her green dress and black coat at no more than four and a half guineas, whereas his Aunt's stylish purple two-piece, lavishly trimmed with cocoa-dyed fox, had, as all the family was aware, cost her ten. Still, that's to be expected, he thought, for the world's a different place to what it used to be. What with radio, combustion engines, aeroplanes, we've speeded things up, made it a place for live progressive men to live in, elbowed out the half-wits. Whatever's Gwen marrying that chap for? he wondered; she could have taken her pick from half a dozen smart young fellows. Me, for instance. *My* wife won't patronise the in-expensive department when it's time for her to fit herself out for *her* son's wedding. . . .

Patricia and Hugh had arrived with no time to spare.

Hugh's morning coat, when located at last in the bottom drawer of the chest of drawers in the spare bedroom, had been practically buttonless. He smelled strongly of camphor, looked elderly, Patricia thought, as, unconscious of the critical glance bent on her, she preceded him into the pew, and quaint. As she dropped on her knees – while Hugh severely seated himself – the loud new organ, reluctantly presented by parishioners and sightseers, burst into praise, and rising she saw her two tall sons standing at the chancel steps. Giles was looking nervous; he glanced about him; a lock of his thick black hair had fallen over his brow. But August was the perfect bridegroom. His large blue eyes gazed expectantly over the heads of the congregation; every strand of his short fair hair was in place and glossy; he had his look of having recently emerged from a hot bath after a day in the open air. Oh, August, thought Patricia, dear brave generous stupid August, what was he waiting for . . . not for the answer to dreams, not even for the brief ecstatic fulfilment of mid-summer madness, but for the journey back when the music has ceased and the dance is over, for the dustcart after the Lord Mayor's show. Or wasn't he? From August's candid face you couldn't tell. . . .

Heads turned. The deafening organ shouted; the choir, smelling of hair oil, passed her; Gwen, invisible under the clouds of her white veil, strutted on her father's arm. Her dress was of good quality white satin sewn with pearl beads; her train was carried by her little cousin, Douglas, a curly-headed child dressed in a 'Bubbles' suit, who was breathing stertorously through well-developed adenoids. Then came Nicola, side by side with Gwen's best girl friend, Dulcie Small,

✱ ✱ ✱

Nicola in mauve and gold taffeta, upholstered and absurd. Her charm had fled. Her thin shoulders looked gawky. There was gooseflesh, Patricia noticed, on her arms. . . .

The organ ceased. The Reverend Mr Rodgers stepped forward. Patricia prayed at last, oh, God, do stop them . . . let there be an impediment . . . let the roof fall in. . .

But there was no impediment and the Norman pillars stood stoutly, being themselves well and truly builded and maintaining that you shall reap as you have sown. Bessie Parker, having satisfied herself that after all Gwen's suspenders hadn't laddered her stockings, and that her shoulder straps didn't show, began to weep quietly into her smart lace-edged handkerchief, while August loudly and clearly and Gwen in a modest whisper took their vows. Giles dropped the ring. With a bright little tinny sound it spun on the brasses and fat Dulcie stooped and retrieved it and with a roguish smile handed it back to Giles. '*With this ring I thee wed*,' spoke up August. '*With my body I thee worship and with all my worldly goods I thee endow. . . .*'

And he's got seven pounds thirteen and three-pence in the post office and a job in the offing, thought Patricia; and he's had all she's got to offer him. There are no goods and there's no worship: only the ring and the trapped years. And Giles talks of perfect truth! Poor young fool, she thought, talking and talking, running here and there, energising, enthusing and all three thousand years too late. . . .

But the Reverend Cyril Rodgers didn't think so. His interminable address was mostly inaudible, but now and then Patricia caught a phrase from some world of his own: you had your ups and downs; you couldn't live always on the heights, but trust and charity (not inertia, dislike of publicity, pity or passion as often as not outlasting respect and admiration) would enable you to support the married state until the day broke and the shadows fled away. Rather a dismal prospect, thought Patricia; such rare virtues needed; and then she became aware that across the aisle Mrs Parker with nods and becks was signalling her towards the vestry. She poked Hugh, who was reading the Thirty-Nine Articles with an outraged expression.

Two pews on the opposite side of the aisle had emptied and the vestry seemed very full of good-humoured prosperous people. With nudges they made way for Patricia. August had signed his name in the clear small handwriting which, Hugh maintained, was all he had learned at Rugby, and Gwen, blushing and giggling, was in the act of signing hers.

'Hullo, Mummy,' said August over the head of a fat Parker relation who was squealing with laughter to see Gwen write her married name. 'What did you think of Giles's *faux pas*? Bad show, I think,' he added chattily. 'What would have happened if we hadn't found the ring?'

Mrs Parker chipped in, 'Some lady in the congregation would have lent one.'

'But nobody can ever get them off,' objected August. 'At least not without soap. Here's Mummy, Gwen.'

'Oh, Mrs Lindsay,' said Gwen and with a little giggle turned her cheek. Patricia bent forward and pecked at it, inhaling a scent that she felt sure was advertised as tantalising. Hugh, who had been standing beside her, moved away.

'Now duck,' said Mrs Parker, 'let Mother arrange your veil.' Twitching the clouds into place, she twittered directions. 'Mrs Lindsay, will you walk down the aisle with Mr Parker and the Professor with me. Then Uncle Bert with Auntie Maud, and Win with Perce and Jack, dear, you take Auntie Flo.'

'*Must* we process?' said Hugh.

'Oh yes,' said Mrs Parker. 'We must do things in style.'

'Well,' said Mr Parker, offering an arm to Patricia, 'the ladies will have their way. . . .'

So, with the organ bellowing behind them, they walked down the aisle and out into the sunshine and when the string of smart hired limousines had rolled away, Hugh brought up their shabby car and Patricia got in and sat down with a sigh and lit a cigarette and said nothing. Hugh, crashing his gears, said, 'Well, if I were a Christian I should have been ashamed to be present at that ceremony,' and then he said, 'They ought to have been married at a register office. Silly of them to draw attention to the date. I suppose they'll call it a seven months' child.'

Patricia said, 'You're very worldly all of a sudden, Hugh.'

Hugh said, why was that worldly, and Patricia explained, 'Well, you seem to know how to go on.' She felt limp, past feeling. The loud sound of the organ still hummed in her ears.

After a corner or two, Hugh had lost sight of the limousines. He drove round and round and finally Patricia had to get out and enter a shop and ask the way to Abbatoirs Street. They found it at last. The little corner house was choc-a-bloc and humming like an agitated beehive, but with perseverance they made their way up the stairs into the pink and green drawing-room above the shop. Mrs Parker, perspiring near the door, apologised. 'A dreadful crush, Mrs Lindsay, and even then it's only relations – we haven't room in our little house for half our friends. Mr Parker wanted to have it in a hotel, he said he could well afford to, but Gwen said no. "Mum," she said, "I'd rather have fewer people and have them in my own home." That's what she said. Shows what kind of a girl she is, doesn't it? Those were her words. "Mum, I'd sooner have fewer people and have them in my own home." That's what she said. Nice, wasn't it? She's changing now, Mrs Lindsay. Lovely she's going to look in her travelling dress. Rust trimmed with green and ever such a saucy hat. It was a pity you weren't here in time to see them cut the cake. Three tiers. Would you care for some refreshment? Downstairs in the dining-room. Here's Sidney. He'll take you. Oh, Sid, take Professor and Mrs Lindsay down.'

Sidney Parker was the family comedian. He clicked his heels together, saluted and said, 'Happy to oblige.' Out in the passage he said to Patricia, 'Say, sister, do I call you Auntie now?'

Patricia said, 'I'm afraid I didn't catch your name.'

'Parker by name but not by nature,' said Sidney humourously fingering his nose. 'But Sidney to you, madam. Or quite simply, Sid.'

Hugh, coming down the stairs behind them, made an odd choked sound. Patricia said, 'If you're Gwen's cousin, I'm afraid I can't claim you for a nephew,' and, turning into the dining-room saw with relief over a small rough sea of hats

Giles's dark head and Nicola's nut-brown one. She made her way towards Giles.

'Now what can I offer you?' said Sidney still at her elbow. 'The wine that is bubbly?'

'Well, just a spot,' said Patricia.

Sidney capered off. Hugh came and stood beside her, saying nothing to her but apologising when people bumped into him. Giles was nearby. At parties he was usually quiet and charming but today he was evidently taking pains to be not snobbish and was carrying on a noisy back-slapping conversation with Stanley Higgins. Nicola in a corner was talking earnestly to a tough-looking man with black crinkly hair and a leathery complexion. In a lull in the general chatter Patricia heard her say 'super-charged' and 'three litre'. Oh, that was good of Nicola. . . . She had got manners. . . . In spite of her dislike of machinery, she was talking about cars. . . .

Sidney returned crying 'Mind yer backs!' like a porter and carrying three glasses of champagne. He toasted, 'The Blushing Bride.' The wine was over-sweet to Patricia's taste but drinking champagne by daylight reminded her of other weddings – Angela and Victor, hopeless Edwardians, idling away their lives against their backcloth of white pillars and ultramarine ocean, figures of fun now for sharp wits, graceful anachronisms even to those who cared for them; herself and Hugh . . . a mad wedding, all for love, and then the long yoked journey and the light going and the nightingales falling silent and the roses dropping one by one. Did it really matter whom you married? Of course it did. Her hand touched Hugh's. You never forgot those days when life blossomed. The blossom fell; the fruit was gathered; the trees stood bare; but hew them, split them, saw them, burn them, and still about your winter rooms there'd be the honeyed smell of that dead spring time. . . . Poor August!

Someone said, 'They're going!' and there was a rush for the door. Hugh, making way, stepped back into the grate and knocked over the 'companion set' of fire-irons. Kneeling down with a little middle-aged grunt, he picked up the stand and laboriously replaced brush, poker and tongs. Patricia on her long legs was tall enough to see, over hats, Gwen and August coming down the stairs. Gwen in a rust-coloured dress and a fox fur was giggling. She had a green gloved hand to her saucy rust-coloured hat. August hadn't bought a new suit to go away in. For a bridegroom he looked a little shabby, and he looked tired and, as Giles might have said if he hadn't been changed and unable to harbour unkind thoughts, definitely not 'pukka sahib'. But he caught Patricia's eye and was instantly smiling. 'Goodbye,' he shouted. 'Love to all. Write soon. Kiss baby from me.'

Gwen had smart new luggage, of shiny scarlet cloth. It was put into the limousine. Then August's battered leather suitcase was carried out, and, waving and laughing under a storm of confetti, Gwen and August got in. The car slid away. It had 'Newly Married' written in white chalk on the back and an old shoe bumped and swung behind.

Patricia turned back to Hugh. He had completed his repairs to the companion set and was standing with his hands in his pockets looking at a firescreen of mirror glass ornamented by painted sprays of flowers.

Patricia said, 'Let's collect Giles and Nicola and go.'

Giles and Nicola were on the doorstep. Nicola fetched her brown tweed coat. It was much too short to cover her trailing frills.

They got into their car. Hugh drove; Patricia sat beside him and Giles and Nicola behind.

'Well,' said Giles, 'that's over. I must say I enjoyed it.'

'Enjoyed it?' echoed Patricia.

'Why not?' said Giles. 'Oh, I suppose . . . But don't you see it's part of God's plan for August?'

Nicola said, 'Do tell me, Giles: is wearing this beastly mauve frock part of God's plan for me?'

'Of course it is,' said Giles. 'That's what makes it so simple. I mean, if you'd realised that and trusted, you wouldn't have been . . . well, out of temper all day.'

'There's one good thing,' Nicola observed, 'about this Group business – it's made Giles into such a nice polite little boy. Before he was changed he would have said "in a bloody bad temper". Giles, darling, share ten bob with me.'

Since Hugh did nothing Patricia said, 'Nicola, do leave it alone. This isn't the Middle Ages. Besides, they like being persecuted. And Giles, do stop saving us.'

'I'm not,' said Giles. 'It's only that – well, supposing you'd come into a fortune, you'd want to tell us about it, wouldn't you?'

'But it isn't a fortune – worse luck,' said Nicola.

'Of course it isn't. That was only a very inadequate analogy. It's so much more than any fortune. . . .'

'Question,' said Nicola.

***

'Oh, Nicola, you're blah – as mad as the rest of them. Look at you all, running round in circles, making money, exchanging it for absurd unnecessary objects and never wondering why. Don't you feel you're in the dark? Don't you want to know the purpose of it all?'

'My dear child,' said Patricia, 'if she did, she wouldn't come to you.'

Hugh at the wheel heard them. He wished that Patricia wouldn't go on clucking, clucking and calling like a hen that doesn't realise her chickens are full grown. *Let the long contention cease! Geese are swans and swans are geese,* he thought, but didn't think on to the next verses because, taking the long view, what fortress was there worth storming . . . ? All these causes on which men had lavished soul and body, what were they now? A paragraph . . . a footnote . . . dusty forgotten things. . . .

CHAPTER ELEVEN

Nicola

I

'Is there *anything* one could do to it?' said Nicola.

'It could be shortened and you could wear it at garden parties. But I don't really think that mauve suits you. Personally I should make it into a nightdress case,' said Patricia.

'I don't think I want a mauve nightdress case,' sighed Nicola.

'You could give it away. Or make it into lavender bags for Christmas presents.'

'Nobody wants lavender bags. Besides, I hate sewing.'

'Well, wear it out at your dancing lesson.'

Nicola, staring into the fire, said, 'I say, if I don't pass Matric. need I try for it again? Couldn't I leave school at the end of summer term?'

'Well,' said Patricia, 'I suppose it depends on what you mean to do afterwards. Personally, unless you're going to teach or be a doctor or something, I don't see much use in these exams.'

✱ ✱ ✱

Nicola was silent and Patricia, pausing at the end of a purl row, glanced at her, saw the pale young profile shaded by the heavy sweep of smooth brown hair. Nicola had no colour, no sparkle, but her features were quite perfect – the straight forehead, the proud little nose, the short upper lip, curved mouth and rounded chin. All very well to talk of sparkling eyes, heart-shaped faces, dimples and curls, but this was a face that time wouldn't alter; it was a face of which one would never tire. . . .

'What do you want to do?' said Patricia, ceasing to tap her teeth with her knitting needle and beginning a plain row. It was pleasant, she thought, sitting here in the schoolroom, girls together, with Nicola. She was glad that she had been extravagant and, instead of going to sit in the library, where Hugh would have shushed every time they spoke, had lit the schoolroom fire.

'Well . . . !' hesitated Nicola.

'Something with horses, wasn't it?' said Patricia encouragingly. 'There are several ways of setting about that, you know. I mean, you could go as pupil teacher sort of arrangement to a riding school, or if you don't want to teach riding you could go to a stud farm. Or we've plenty of room here. I thought of that when I first saw the place. I used to know something about horses and I daresay it would soon come back to me. I could help you if you'd like to start breeding children's ponies, or breaking them, right away.'

Nicola said nothing. She seemed to be pondering. Patricia, setting aside all that it would mean to her if, now that August and Giles were deserters, Nicola came to live at home,

✷ ✷ ✷

said brightly, 'But anyhow I expect it would be more amusing for you – and better perhaps – if you got some experience first in a place where there were other girls.'

Nicola said, 'But I don't think I'm much use with horses.'

'You're not bad,' said Patricia. 'You've got a good seat and fair hands. After all, you haven't had much chance with only Griselda.'

'I know,' said Nicola. 'But everyone says the same thing – a seat and hands are all very nice but there's much more to it. I know I look all right and I don't fall off or anything, but there are lots of girls who are always coming off and look like nothing on earth, yet they can do anything with horses. I couldn't make a pony jump if it didn't want to, and they don't want to with me. And anyhow I've come to the conclusion that I'm not frightfully keen. Look at August: he's quite happy standing for hours in the stable communing with Griselda, and he says his guts turn over when he hears a hound speak. Mine don't. You know, Mummy, what I should really like would be to do something with cars.'

Patricia said faintly, 'Cars?'

'Yes,' said Nicola. 'But I don't quite know how. I mean, they don't have girls in garages.'

'But Nicola,' said Patricia, 'isn't this only because you've just learned to drive? I know it's exciting at first but when you get used to it, there's simply nothing in it. You just go out and switch on and step on a self-starter and off you go. Then it's no more exciting than walking or riding a bicycle. . . .'

'But, Mummy, it's not only driving. There's all the mechanical part.'

150

'But that's not interesting. It's only a few bits of tin screwed together. A car doesn't love you. It doesn't whinny when it hears your footstep. It hasn't got a mind.'

'Well, I can't help it,' said Nicola. 'I love them. After all, Mummy, lots of people do.'

'Only nit-wits,' said Patricia.

'I don't think that's fair. Nobody could be more nit-witted than the hunting crowd.'

Patricia said, 'Nonsense. What about Patrick Chalmers and Siegfried Sassoon?'

Nicola said again, 'Well, I can't help it. I'm made like that. After all, you did ask me what I wanted to do.'

Patricia's knitting lay neglected in her lap. In her mind's eye she saw horses: little grey Charity standing patiently under the oaks while she practised vaulting on; bright bay Flavia, the lovely light-weight hunter that her grandfather had given her on her fourteenth birthday, cantering up to the park railings for carrots with the wind in her mane and the sun on her shining flanks, so perfect in movement, so lovely in form that you felt that lift of the heart towards heaven that another might feel hearing music, at the sight of soaring snow-peaks or boundless sea; big brown Truth, Lord Waveney's favourite, waiting at covertside, head up, ears pricked, trembling a little; Black August, epitome of power and courage, thundering down the straight to win. There was the sky in those pictures; there was the wind and the smell of grass; there was shivering and sweating in them; there was being fearless and being afraid. But Nicola didn't want them. Well, turn over. Smell petrol. Smell plush. See the wheels roll and the easy miles go by. There was skill in it, of course, and there was power and speed but how did you get them? You went out with a full pocket and bought them, you fat white woman, you paunchy financier; and the deal was over. You didn't need courage or patience or gentleness, a tempered mind or hardened body to enjoy your man-made thing. . . .

'I know I did,' said Patricia, 'and of course I meant you to say. It's no use spending your life doing something you don't like, so we'll wash out horses. . . . But all the same I think whatever you do with cars it's a barren job to choose.'

'How do you mean?'

'Well, what good do you do? I mean, in some jobs you serve the State and in some humanity. I suppose anyone who teaches feels that he's serving the young and even people who write novels can look back at the end of their lives and think, well, anyhow, they tried to amuse. . . .'

'Oh – service,' said Nicola in contemptuous tones. 'We hear a lot about that at school. But what's the use of it? Nobody's grateful. Look at retired Colonels! Everyone laughs at them and they're always poor. Can't I leave school at the end of the summer, Mummy, and take a course at some motor school? Then perhaps I could get a job as a chauffeuse.'

'Does anybody want chauffeuses?'

'Oh yes, some people do. Nervous old ladies who are afraid of men. Or you get a job driving a cake shop van.'

'Well, I'll talk to your father,' said Patricia. 'I don't suppose he'll mind. The only thing is he may be awkward about your leaving school. . . .'

II

Hugh didn't mind. When Patricia said, 'Nicola wants to do something with cars,' he said, 'Oh yes. I've noticed she drives very well.'

Patricia said, 'Somehow I never thought that any of them cared for machines.'

Hugh said with no regret, 'Well, this is a mechanical age.'

Patricia said, 'I told her I thought it was a barren sort of job. I mean, at the end of it all, what good will she have done?'

'None whatever,' said Hugh. 'But it's the same with everything. Look at me, standing up on my hind legs and lecturing, probably quite erroneously, to a roomful of young men who aren't listening. What good have I done? Just lived and buzzed a bit, that's all.'

'Oh, Hugh, how futile!'

'Futility, thy name is man,' said Hugh.

Patricia didn't believe that. In the first place she had hope of heaven; in the second place she didn't want to believe that all the struggle you'd had, all the virtue you'd put into it just went for nothing, that you bore children and raised them and they just buzzed and were gone. It wasn't a woman's philosophy and she hated it and in reaction flew to Giles.

But Giles was no comfort. He said that he didn't think Nicola was simply out for pleasure – the pleasure of speed and so on – or for a cushy job; he'd always suspected that she had a mechanical mind. He said, 'Do trust God a bit. I'm sure this is part of His plan for her'; and he said, 'All this anxiety is so senseless. If you'd only just listen to God . . .' Patricia said tartly that she could hear all that any Sunday at Church, and Giles said, of course, but why not bring it right into her life? Patricia couldn't answer because she did believe that He counts His sparrows but she certainly didn't trust Him to look after Nicola. Giles saw his chance and pressed her. Wouldn't she come to tea in his rooms next term and meet a few of his friends and hear what they had to say? Patricia said no, she didn't think she would, and Giles said, wasn't that rather unlike her; he meant, wasn't it rather refusing things?

That stung Patricia. She said, 'All right. Next term . . .'

CHAPTER TWELVE

Giles

I

Giles's room was touchingly familiar. In the armchairs and on the sofa were the off-white printed linen cushions that she had sewn for him; over the mantelpiece was the Derain reproduction which had hung in the school room at Hodson's Pightle till Giles had persuaded August, who'd wanted a hunting crop, and Nicola, who'd wanted a wireless, to sell their share of it to him; the curtains were a pair that she'd had in her bedroom at Glasgow – she had counted the squiggles on them when Nicola was being born. Odd, she thought, saying yes . . . yes, to a young man who was telling her about the rotation of crops in East Anglia; odd how familiar the room was when it was really the room of a stranger. For Giles, walking round offering cakes, beaming, making little emasculated jokes, wasn't the boy she'd raised. Her Giles was the boy who had wanted to climb Everest. . . .

'As a matter of fact,' said Patricia with asperity, 'I was brought up in that part of the world – at a place called Hulver.'

'Oh really?' said the young man, who had been introduced as Robin. 'Actually, that's rather queer. When I was down there I went to lunch with the Rector of South Moreton. The church is in Lord Waveney's park and the Rector was appealing for money to restore some stonework òn the tower – it's Norman and too divine – but no one would give a penny. I suggested that we should pray for a miracle – why not? – but he wouldn't, so I did, and a few days later he found in his mail a cheque for a hundred pounds from Lord Waveney.'

A tough-looking lad in a check coat and a sporting tie had been listening to the conversation. He said, 'Well, I'll tell you something.' Robin put in, 'This is Henry,' and Henry went on, 'Before I was changed I never could get up in the morning. Of course that made trouble . . .' His reminiscences were cut short by Giles, who, standing with his back to the fireplace, announced in a clear voice that if everyone had finished tea, some people were going to share their experiences. 'I'll lead off,' said Giles and without a trace of shyness but with smiles and beams began to tell how difficult he had always been at home, how he had never been able to get on with his elder brother; how morose he'd been, going out for long walks by himself, struggling with all sorts of imaginary difficulties. Then he'd met someone – his friend, Peter, a most wonderful fellow, whom he hoped they'd all meet one day, and, coming home from a climbing expedition in the most marvellous sunset, Peter had said to him quite casually, 'By the way, has God any place in your life, Giles?' Of course Giles had been taught the usual things, had been confirmed at school and so on, but nobody had ever said anything like that to him – quite casually, coming back from a climbing expedition, 'Has God any place in your life, Giles?' Of course he'd realised at once that in spite of endless chapels and being confirmed and so on, God hadn't any place *in his life*, and he had had to admit it to Peter. They had had some marvellous talks and Giles had seen how absolutely different his life might be, but for a long time he had hesitated to join the Group for the most absurd reason – fear! For ages he'd been afraid to tell his people! Of course that wasn't being changed. The change came later. He'd prayed for a miracle – why not? – and on the afternoon of the same day he walked out into the country to have tea with his people, and quite suddenly, when he was in the orchard collecting eggs with his mother, he found that it was perfectly simple to tell her, and he did, and then of course he knew that he was properly changed. And now everything was quite different. He was happy at home and he never had any unkind thoughts about his elder brother. He never wanted to go for long walks by himself but always with someone else so that he could share everything – the landscape, his thoughts and so on. And another thing. Before he'd been changed he'd been snobbish, noticed when people were, well, what the last generation would have called 'not quite'. But now it was all different. He'd been to a show the other day – his brother's wedding actually – and there were lots of people like that there, and he hadn't thought of anything except what awfully charming people they were. And now would somebody else say something, please, as he was sure they were all tired of him.

Giles sat down and Henry rose from Patricia's side and said that he would like to say a few words, and Giles said that that was Henry and if they didn't all know him they'd heard of his father, Lord Croftmore. Henry went across to the fireplace and said that before he'd been changed he'd been a poor sort of fellow. He couldn't get up in the mornings; he went to cocktail parties and drank too much and he was sorry to say that in his relations with girls he hadn't always been too pure. Of course after he was changed it was all quite different. He got up, took the dogs out before breakfast, didn't touch drink or think any more about girls. His people had asked what on earth was the matter with him, so he'd told them, and they'd laughed at first, but he'd just carried on and now everyone in the house was changed, even the kitchenmaid. It just showed, didn't it? Well . . . he thought that was all he'd got to say.

Henry sat down and Giles said, 'What Henry's said is awfully interesting. I mean, it just shows what's happening. His people laughed, but this thing's infectious. They laughed but it spread right through the house even down to the kitchenmaid. I mean, it's a revolution. And now Pamela's going to speak. I think you all know Pamela or else you know her people. Her father's Lord Sonning.'

Pamela took Giles's place. She was a big fresh-faced girl with large teeth. She wore a well-cut grey coat and skirt and a silver fox fur was slung over her broad shoulders giving the impression of a successful return from the chase. Spraying out saliva because her lips didn't quite cover her teeth, she said that she hadn't been like Giles and Henry – she'd been perfectly happy at home and her parents were the dearest old

* * *

things on earth but what had happened was that she had kept on falling in love – only of course it wasn't love – with every single young man who came to Sonning Abbots. It had been most awfully awkward and really very exhausting, and then one day a young man had come to the house and, as it had turned out, he was a member of the Group and instead of the usual nonsense they had had a most marvellous talk and the result had been that she had been changed too, and since then she had met hundreds and hundreds of young men and never fallen in love – but of course it wasn't love – once. But she hadn't been so successful as Henry. She had asked her father and mother to give God a trial but so far they hadn't. However, one must just carry on, as Henry said, and one bright spot was that she'd changed the chauffeur. He'd always been a perfect nuisance and rather inclined to take liberties but now he was quite different. He came in every morning to her little sitting-room and they had their Quiet Time together – wasn't it splendid? She'd have brought him today to speak for himself only she'd had to drive the little car because her mother had wanted the Rolls for shopping – that was the extraordinary thing about people who weren't changed: they gave such a lot of time and thought to little things like buying a hat but they couldn't spare a moment to listen to God. That was all, she thought, except that she would like to say what a help it had been to hear about Henry's people laughing and then being changed after all. Of course, as Giles had said, it was a revolution – people couldn't stand up to it. That really was all, except that sharing like this was such a help. She meant that living among people who weren't changed was

159

rather difficult, but of course it wasn't so bad as being crucified – they must all remember that. Now that *was* all. . . .

Pamela sat down and Giles said had anybody else got anything to say or any questions to ask? No one apparently had, so, after waiting a few moments he said, 'No? Well, I hope you'll all stay on a bit . . . Henry, I want you to meet Sylvia . . .' Everybody got up and stood about again in groups talking and a dark girl in horn-rimmed glasses, who had been sitting behind Patricia, said to her, 'Do you think one could go?'

'Yes,' said Patricia. 'I'm going to fade as soon as I've said goodbye to Giles.'

'Robin Herriot brought me,' said the spectacled girl. 'But if I spoke to him now, I'd only give him a raspberry . . . I think all this is foul.'

Patricia's diffused feelings crystallised. She said, 'Sickening, isn't it?' and went across the room to Giles.

Giles said, 'Oh, you're not *going*?'

'I must,' said Patricia. 'The hens . . .'

As soon as she'd said it she remembered Pamela's mother, who took endless time and trouble over shopping but hadn't a moment to spare for listening to God, but Giles only said, 'Oh, bother the hens,' and then, 'Well, I'll see you out. Don't go anybody.' He walked across the room with Patricia and on the landing with the fire buckets in a row and a gramophone downstairs playing *Wein, Weib und Gesang*, he said, 'Well, what did you think of it?'

Patricia said, 'Well, Giles, I don't want to hurt your feelings but I must say I thought you all awfully girlish.'

'Girlish?'

* * *

'Yes. You know your Aunt Angela and I used to lie in bed and tell each other all the naughty things we'd done. If one hadn't done any, one invented. It was great fun.'

Giles said, 'But we aren't children.'

'No,' said Patricia, 'but you're awfully young. It's not a revolution, Giles. You might call it a youth movement and I shouldn't mind that because youth movements don't last, can't last, because youth doesn't. Don't take this too seriously, Giles; don't spend too much time on it because you'll get over it.'

'You've got me all wrong,' said Giles.

He stood pushing a finger up and down on the old black oak banister, looking over her head through the long staircase window. Patricia looked too, and saw chestnut trees in flower and the blue sky and a bird flying. 'So awful,' she said, 'on a day like this, stuffing indoors and talking about your souls.'

To be accused of stuffing indoors had always irritated Giles. He burst out, 'That *would* be your line. But we're not always talking. We're doing. Oh, I know you wouldn't call it doing. Doing to you is building bridges, drilling soldiers.'

Patricia said, 'Well – have you ever read "The Sons of Martha"?'

'Kipling,' said Giles with scorn.

'Yes,' said Patricia, and it was no use arguing so she said, 'Well, I must be off, my dear. And anyhow thank you for my nice tea.'

She went downstairs and across the quad. Birds were singing. The afternoon sun threw the blue shadows of pinnacles across the grass. She took a deep breath. Probably

＊ ＊ ＊

Hugh was right; it was only a phase, but chestnut flowers and maytime don't last for ever. Why didn't they come out and play, those silly children . . .?

The next morning Patricia received a letter from Giles. He wrote: *Dear Mummy, after you had left I had some unkind thoughts about you. I am sorry. Will you forgive your loving Giles?*

CHAPTER THIRTEEN

✽ ✽ ✽

August

I

August had written once from Torquay. He had said that the weather was fine and the hotel quite comfortable. He wrote again during May from a private hotel in West Kensington. He had found a job at last as a salesman in Sempercool Limited. It wasn't touting – a proper appointment was made in reply to enquiries, and if you did well there was a good chance of an executive position. He was to start work on Monday – wasn't it thrilling? – and, as even cheap hotels worked out so expensive, he and Gwen had taken a tiny house in South Wimbledon. It was only a tiny house, of course; they were only paying eighteen and sixpence a week for it; you paid eighteen and sixpence a week and then after so many years you had bought it. They were going to furnish it on the hire purchase system – everyone did nowadays – and, if it wouldn't be a bother, would Patricia send along the things that belonged to him? There was the mask and the pad and his pictures – they would do for his dressing-room, and any of his old clothes that were lying about would do for gardening. . . .

* * *

Later on in the morning Patricia went upstairs to August's bedroom. August wasn't like Giles: beyond liking old things better than new and no colour as well as hunting yellow, he had never had any ideas on furnishing or decoration. When they had moved into Hodson's Pightle Patricia had had all the rooms and passages distempered white, but the next year Giles had painted his walls a dim pale green and the year after a deep shiny yellow, and before he had become absorbed in his Group activities he had been talking of a striped Regency paper. His pictures had changed too. He had cast out Micky and Cracker for the Acropolis and the Acropolis for Nanga Parbat and Nanga Parbat for Degas, and Patricia had said was he a straw in the wind? but Hugh had said no, it was all right; he was feeling his way. August hadn't apparently felt his way for his walls were still white, and ornamented as they'd always been with the Quorn in full cry and Minoru winning the Derby.

Patricia got out the old trunk which August used to take to school and his battered private-school playbox. She packed Minoru and the Quorn and the wooden hounds from the mantelpiece and the mask and the pad, and then she dried her eyes and went downstairs and suggested to Hugh that they should let August have the oak chest-of-drawers with the lion-head handles and the Cromwellian dressing-table. Hugh demurred but Patricia reminded him of Blanche and the pestles and mortars and the twelve darned damask tablecloths, so he gave in and Patricia went round the house and collected various objects that he'd never miss – a Persian rug, a quilted cushion, a cut glass whisky decanter and so

✳ ✳ ✳

on – and she had them all dispatched to 'Restholme', Bloomhurst Avenue, SW20. August wrote gratefully telling her that the weather was fine and they were settled in now and Gwen said would she come and stay a night with them; and Patricia wrote back that she couldn't stay just now because of the young chickens but she would drive over one Saturday and have tea.

Garden parties, the big end of the car and haymaking delayed her and it was July before she went. August had drawn her a map of South Wimbledon but she lost her way, muddled Morden and Merton, was three times misdirected, and arrived hot, confused and frantic in Bloomhurst Avenue. It was a new road, pock-marked with pot-holes, sunk between banks which were soberly carpeted with dead grass. On the top of the banks ran footpaths along which smartly dressed young women were dragging fatigued toddlers; and gimcrack houses started at each other across the abyss.

Patricia stopped the car, ascended the bank and began a systematic search for 'Restholme'. After walking the whole length of the footpath on one side she realised that though August had explained that his house was on the right, her peregrinations round Morden and Merton had brought her into the avenue from the opposite end. She crossed the road and saw 'Restholme' painted in archaic letters on the first little gate to which she came.

It was a neat little house, white with green paint on the front door, windows and gables. The front garden had been dug and sown with grass, which was doing well in patches.

The little gate wouldn't open.

Patricia pushed at it and the whole fence swayed. Then she saw that the hinges had dropped, so she lifted it. Without a protest the hinges and their screws parted company with the woodwork.

Patricia set the gate down, thumped the screws home with her fist, walked up the curling pathway and rang the electric bell. The bakelite fitting was loose on the stucco and a slight electric shock went tingling up her fingers. She waited for some moments noticing that the jamb of the door had warped away from the wood leaving a half-inch gap, and was summoning up courage to ring again when she heard the click of high heels and the door opened.

'Oh, Mrs Lindsay, I'd nearly given you up.'

Gwen was dressed in a smart black afternoon frock with a big white pleated collar. Her colour was high; her eyes were bright; her hair was smooth and shiny. In her blue linen dress and straw hat Patricia felt faded.

She apologised for being late. Gwen said, 'Do come in. David had to go to Worcester Park to see a prospect – such a shame on a Saturday. He hoped to see you before he went, but he'll be back directly. Come into our lounge. I do hope you'll like it.'

It was a very purple room. There was a purple carpet and two armchairs, which were dun-coloured but each furnished with a round cushion of purple silk. The sofa was purple and the three cushions on it were dun-coloured. The curtains were purple. The walls and the hearthrug were dun. The tiled fireplace, round which the cement was cracking, needed no fender, but there was a companion set of dazzling brass fire-irons. A cabinet radio-gramophone stood against the wall opposite the fireplace. There were no pictures in the room.

Gwen said, 'Modern, isn't it? David wanted something lighter but those wishy-washy shades have gone out, you know. Do sit down. You'll find the couch quite comfortable, and I'll bring in the trolley. We won't wait for David. I can make fresh tea for him.'

Patricia, intimidated by the splendour of the cushions, sat down on the sofa's edge, and in a moment a tea trolley appeared with Gwen smiling behind it. 'Modern, isn't it?' she said, 'and how do you like our tea service? Original, isn't it? Mum had a fit when she saw it.' It was a white tea service bordered with green. The tea-cups had solid handles. The teapot was square.

'It makes a nice cup of tea,' said Gwen pouring out. 'Of course, you know tea's coming in again. Do have a plate, Mrs Lindsay, and a tea knife and here's a serviette, for you. Aren't they dainty? My girl friend, Dulcie Small – I expect you remember her as my other bridesmaid – sweet she looked, didn't she? – she worked these.'

Patricia examined a small mauve flower, and said, 'I see they match the room.'

'Well,' said Gwen, 'she knew that I liked mauve. But it's not quite the shade. A bit wishy-washy. Do have a sandwich, Mrs Lindsay. Egg and cress or cucumber. I made them myself, so you needn't be afraid.'

The sandwiches were neatly piled on lace d'oylies. Patricia took one.

'How do you like the neighbourhood?'

✳ ✳ ✳

'Oh, I love it. All the people are such good class and there are a lot of other newly-marrieds. David said there wouldn't be anyone to know but I've made heaps of friends already – good class people but not a bit stand-offish. And it's so nice being in a new house – it's lovely to know that it's all new and clean and no one's lived here before. I shouldn't fancy an old house. And we've got all the latest gadgets. I do like electric cooking – no dust or dirt – and when Baby comes I'm going to have an electric washer, too.'

Patricia asked, 'Do you want a boy or a girl?'

'Oh, a girl, Mrs Lindsay. You can dress them so much daintier.'

Patricia had a sudden devastating vision of her first grand-child, a daintily dressed infant with black ringlets and a high colour, growing up among good class people and the amenities of electricity, August's daughter and growing up in Bloomhurst Avenue. If August had married Elspeth . . . she saw a disreputable imp galloping a shaggy pony round an orchard in the rain. . . .

Gwen said, starting up, 'There's David! Excuse me, Mrs Lindsay. I always like to be at the door to welcome him in.'

She ran out. Patricia heard August say, 'That damned rickety little gate's come off its hinges again.'

Gwen said, 'Naughty boy to swear,' and then she said, 'Do remember to wipe your feet, dear. You know how every mark shows on the lounge carpet.' There was the dry bristling sound of August wiping his dusty shoes and then he came in and said, 'Hullo!'

Patricia said, 'I'm afraid it was me who made the gate come

off its hinges,' and August grinned and said, 'You're not used to coping with twentieth-century workmanship.' He looked pale and tired, she thought, and then she thought no, he didn't. He was as brown as he'd always been, showed no more trace of fatigue than after a day's hunting: it was just that his look of *jeunesse dorée* was gone.

Gwen said, 'You looked fagged out, darling. Sit down and talk to your mother while I make you some nice fresh tea.'

'What's here will do,' said August.

'Indeed it won't,' said Gwen picking up the teapot. 'Only the best is good enough for *my* hubby.'

August said, 'But I like stewed tea.'

'Don't tell stories,' said Gwen, halfway to the door.

'Well, if I *must* have it, let me get it,' said August following her.

'Certainly not,' said Gwen firmly. 'You don't come home to fetch and carry for me.'

She went out. August said, 'She *will* wait on me. I wish she wouldn't.'

He sat down. Patricia said, 'How do you like it here, August?'

'Oh, it's not so bad,' said August cheerfully. 'Of course these houses are nothing but lath and plaster, and it's all cracking and everything's off its hinges already, but they have their advantages; all the electric gadgets make things much easier for Gwen. Of course they go wrong pretty often but still, they don't make dust. And the garden will be nice when we've got things to grow and of course the air's good. It'll be much better than London for the che-ild.'

'And how do you like your work?'

'Oh, it's great fun. All the funny houses one goes to . . . And of course there's a great future in it. People are at last beginning to realise that a refrigerator is not a luxury but a necessity.'

'Is it?'

'Madam,' said August in a shocked voice, 'is it possible that you, a housewife, are not alive to the necessity for proper food preservation? Have you never considered the economy that can be effected by the elimination of needless food spoilage? Can you ignore the fact that during the month of November . . .'

Gwen reappeared.

'Now then, dear. Some nice fresh tea for you. . . . And do try one of my tomato sandwiches.'

'I've finished them,' said August.

'Oh dear,' cried Gwen, 'I *am* so sorry. Mrs Lindsay, I must apologise. You'll think me a terrible housekeeper but really I thought there was ample.'

August said, 'There was. But Mummy wouldn't have another and it's no use leaving them.'

'Oh, but David, dear, you always ought to leave two at least. It's so embarrassing when there's only one to offer.'

'Why?' asked August.

'Well, it makes us look so poor.'

'We *are* poor,' said August.

Gwen's colour rose.

'Even if we are, we should keep up appearances, shouldn't we, Mrs Lindsay?'

Patricia said uncomfortably, 'I can't say I think appearances matter. . . . Do show me the rest of the house, Gwen.'

'I'd love to. How is your cup, David?'

'Fullish,' said August.

'All right then. I'll be back in time to pour out your second.'

At the foot of the little staircase she said to Patricia, 'Will you go first, Mrs Lindsay, or shall I lead the way?' Patricia found herself saying wearily that she didn't mind, so Gwen tripped upstairs before her and opened the door of the front room. 'This is our bedroom.'

There were twin beds spread with pink taffeta and a grey maplewood suite with pink handles. A second door led into August's dressing-room, which was over the porch and rather crowded by his oak furniture.

'Oh, I'm glad that was useful,' said Patricia and went to look at the Quorn in full cry.

'It saved us buying,' Gwen admitted. 'But I did want David to have one of those lovely "Hanganfold" wardrobes.'

'You can always sell it,' said Patricia.

'David wouldn't,' said Gwen. 'He likes old things – funny, isn't it? But I did draw the line at that fox's face. I couldn't bear it.'

The bath was pink marblette and rather small, Patricia thought, for August, but Gwen said no, it was so easy to clean, and passed on to the third room. 'You can guess who's going in here,' she said, 'but so far I've only made the curtains. Take a peep out of the window, Mrs Lindsay, and you'll see the garden. Next year when it's all nice David's promised me a lovely garden lounge.'

Patricia took a peep at the narrow strip between its inexorable fences.

'What are you going to do with it?'

Gwen said, 'David had a mad idea of sowing grass and letting it grow long and planting fruit trees. Like an orchard. Mad, wasn't it? But I said, whatever would people think? so now he's come round and we're going to have some nice crazy paving.'

Yes, thought Patricia, and that's how it'll be for the rest of August's life: whatever will people think? and then he'll come round until he's so used to coming round that he won't have any ideas mad or otherwise to offer; and she saw August, tall, pale, middle-aged with nothing to say. She said, 'You know, Gwen, crazy paving does need a lot of weeding,' but Gwen said, 'Not the concrete sort that's just made to look old-fashioned. That's what everybody has nowadays.'

When they got back to the lounge August had his head in his hands but, hearing the door open, he leaped up and asked if Patricia didn't think it was all very well arranged? Patricia said yes, and they praised the house until she said that she must go.

August walked with her to the car. He said God, he'd like a bathe and Patricia said wasn't there anywhere? and he said no, only swimming baths. Then he asked how Griselda was and Patricia said, 'All right,' and August said, 'Good.'

'She'll last for years,' said Patricia. 'She'll come in useful when you teach the che-ild to ride.'

August said, looking up and down Bloomhurst Avenue, 'I expect it will be rather an urban che-ild.'

* * *

'Oh no,' said Patricia. 'It mustn't be. I shan't allow that. I shall have it to stay. What are you going to call it?'

'I believe that Gwen and her Mum favour Daphne,' said August, opening the door of the car.

'Oh dear,' said Patricia. 'Can't we do something?'

'Nothing, I'm afraid,' said August slamming the door.

'Well,' said Patricia, 'there it is. Cheerio.'

'Goodbye,' said August. 'Come again.'

'I will,' said Patricia and as there was no more to say unless she said everything, she turned the car, waved and drove away.

August stood watching the battered car and he smiled at the dented wings, the rusted number plate and the rather flat tyres. Then he noticed that a piece of straw was caught in the spokes of the spare wheel and he stopped smiling because straw wasn't often to be seen in Bloomhurst Avenue, and it was so awfully like his mother to drive about with straw in her spare wheel, and that particular piece of straw came from Griselda's stable and it had grown green and golden and stood in sheaves in a wide field bordered with elms in Oxfordshire. He shut his eyes and he could see the field: the hedge layered but not up to the standard of the shires; the gate that you could put your weight on and it wouldn't come off its hinges; the ruts that the waggons made as they passed through it; the hoof-prints of the big slow farm horses. The field lay on a southerly slope and the sun soaked it and the soft rains drenched it and by God, the south-west wind could blow there! Below it there was a grass lane, which was probably something to do with the Romans, and above it there was a little wood that was famous for foxes. . . . And all this because of a piece of straw, thought August, opening his eyes and seeing Bloomhurst Avenue; and, trying to swallow back a sudden tightness in his throat, he thought, damn it, why did she come here in her old clothes looking like tea in the garden and we'll bathe when we've digested, why did she come reminding me . . . ?

He went back to the gate, which he had propped against the fence – he must mend it tomorrow or whatever would people think? – and there was Gwen in the garden.

'Well,' she said, 'it passed off all right, didn't it?'

'Yes,' said August.

'Your mother didn't exactly rave,' said Gwen. 'I mean, it wasn't like showing Mum round. I mean, she hadn't much to say, had she?'

'I thought she was doing her best,' said August.

'I did mine, I know that,' said Gwen. 'Still, it takes all sorts to make a world, doesn't it? Now I'm going to change my dress and wash up tea. You look tired, David. You go and sit on the couch in the lounge and read your paper.'

August was tired, but he didn't want to go and sit on the couch in the lounge and read his paper. He wanted to shout, 'Wait for me!' and dash off down Bloomhurst Avenue after the battered car that was going back to Oxfordshire. He'd climb on the running board and get in and Patricia would say, 'Hullo, August,' and drive on and he'd go back, back to fields and trees and hedges and the moon coming up over the lift of the stubble, back to an old house where shifting wood fires made dust on the mantlepieces, where you had dining-room tea and a loaf that you cut for yourself and no d'oylies, back to

* * *

people who didn't mind saying that they were poor or that there was nothing to eat in the house, back to the old loves and the old dreams and hopes and the old way of living. . . .

But it was too late, half a year too late to shout, 'Wait for me,' and dash off down Bloomhurst Avenue. So there was nothing to do but to go into the house and sit on the couch in the lounge and read his paper.

II

Patricia, missing her way, slipping the clutch and wishing she were dead, drove back to Oxfordshire. It's not so bad, he'd said of the house, and it's great fun, he'd said of selling refrigerators, and he'd sat on purple cushions and eaten off d'oylies and he'd known what she was thinking but he had shut a door, a door that said Private No Admittance, between them. It wasn't fair. She'd borne him, nursed him, trundled him, suffered his infant screams, his toddler's whines, his schoolboy humour, his adolescent sulks, but now his loyalty wasn't to her: he could lie to her for Gwen's sake without the flicker of an eyelid. I expect it'll be rather an urban child, he'd said without emotion, and Patricia could see that Gwen had a good wife's stranglehold on him but couldn't see why she herself had no hold, why in all those years and years she had accomplished nothing. Whatever will people think? Gwen had said, and he'd neither laughed her to scorn nor cursed her; round like a weathercock he'd come and she was to have her crazy paving. Oh, it wasn't just a matter of taste: she knew where art gets off, who'd eaten rice pudding and prunes under the Hulver Rubens; but all his life she'd taught August to hate shams, and there he was taking quite kindly and quietly to the villa lie. It would be an urban child. . . . It would say perspiration and lady dog; it would screw up its little nose at mud and the smell of a farmyard; it would pity shepherds, envy film stars; daintily dressed it would walk through life, a pavement between its feet and earth, an umbrella between its head and the sky. And August would let it, he'd stand aside and let it because . . . well, face it . . . he'd never really cared for the things that she had wanted him to care for; like Nicola riding Griselda and saying thank you for books on horse-manship and all the time dreaming of cars, he'd screwed up his eyes and said that the wood had been wild and wet and purplish, but only to please her, so that neither of the virtues she had loved so much in him, neither honesty nor simplicity, seemed to him worth fighting for. . . .

At Slough she had a puncture. At Bix the car boiled. When she got home Hugh said well, after all *he'd* been brought up in a doll's house and look at *him!*

CHAPTER FOURTEEN

A Dull Christmas

I

Nicola came home from school in high spirits. She had found
a job. A relative of her greatest friend kept a florist's shop in
Mayfair and Jane was going to serve in the shop and learn the
business, and Nicola was going to share their flat and drive
the delivery van. That was, of course, if Hugh and Patricia
had no objection. Patricia thought it a poor job with no future,
but Hugh said that didn't matter for a girl – they always got
married: so Nicola spent a month at home dancing with
impatience, only happy when she was tinkering with the car
or driving it or studying a large scale map of London.

Giles went to Holland and when he came back he said that
he didn't want to carry on any longer at Oxford; he'd had
definite Guidance that he was to go with a party of other life-
savers to America. Hugh, roused at last, forbade it, but Giles,
once so sensitive, wouldn't take no. Evening after evening he
argued, citing the disciples to Patricia, pleading for freedom
of thought to Hugh, finally reminding both of them that he'd

be twenty-one in February and able to do as he pleased, so that by compelling him to remain at St Mary's they would merely be making him unhappy and wasting a term's fees. Hugh saw that, and was shaken but still had a shot to fire. 'You can go,' he said, 'but please understand that if you do your allowance automatically ceases; you won't get another penny from me.'

Giles stared at him.

'But I didn't expect it. Money doesn't matter. . . .'

'Don't be silly, Giles,' said Patricia. 'It's no fun to starve.'

Giles said, 'Oh, that's all right. None of us has starved yet. Lots of people have got down to their last shilling and then they've prayed and gone to bed and not worried a bit and in the morning the money was there.'

'Where?' asked Patricia.

'In their letters,' said Giles. 'Or someone blew in. It's perfectly simple. . . .'

'All right,' said Hugh. 'Go to America and try it. And if you do get into a mess and there's nothing in your letters and nobody blows in, you can apply to me and I'll send you your passage money home. But there's a condition to that. If you do apply to me it's understood that you're giving up all this tom-foolery and coming home with the intention of getting a decent job.'

'All right,' said Giles. 'I'll agree to that. But it won't happen. God won't let me down, I know.'

He went to America in December and he wrote home and said that he was having a marvellous time. The enthusiasm there was astounding. It was a revolution, especially among

✻ ✻ ✻

American business men. This was a typical instance: Westrop
P Mappers, whom they might have heard of, had joined the
Group, and he had always sweated his employees, but as soon
as he was changed he had put up the wages in all his factories
and the very next day he had got a perfectly colossal contract
which he'd never even hoped to secure. That was only one
instance, but such things were happening every day. Giles
was staying with Westrop P Mappers. He'd a marvellous home
full of priceless pictures and furniture, and the food was too
wonderful and there was a squash court and a quite incredible
swimming pool. . . .

Hugh said that Giles had had better luck than the
disciples, but when Patricia answered his letter she refrained
from such comments and described small happenings at
home which she thought might touch him: the gale they'd
had just after he left had blown down the Ribston Pippin
that he'd named Edmund Spenser, but had spared the even
more decrepit Dan Chaucer: Griselda had been given away
to the Waneflete children but had known Patricia's step and
whinnied when she had gone there to tea.

Giles was a long time answering her letter and, when he
did, he didn't mention Edmund Spenser or Griselda. He told
her about the marvellous time he was having in Washington
and gave an instance of a Senator who had been changed and
had eschewed bribery and corruption but got himself elected
all the same.

August's baby was born in October. It was, as Gwen had
hoped, a girl, but she had changed her mind about calling it
Daphne; Daphne was sweet but not awfully up to date and the

name that she had now quite definitely decided on was Elizabeth Rose. Patricia went to see her in a nursing home, where she was costing Hugh ten guineas a week and seemed inclined to linger, and she told Patricia what a terrible time she'd had, but never mind, now she'd got Baby; and she said that Patricia needn't fear; she wasn't going to put Baby before Daddy like some girls. Before Patricia left, August appeared carrying a shiny black briefcase and a bowler hat. He kissed Gwen and gave her a bunch of violets and said no, he wasn't tired and yes, business was splendid. Patricia told him that hounds had met that morning at the cross roads and drawn the spinney, and August said, 'Oh,' and then, 'By the way, thanks awfully for the pram. We got a blue one. . . .'

II

It was dull that Christmas. Nicola came home but August and Gwen and Elizabeth Rose couldn't come: the slightest alteration in routine upset Elizabeth Rose's digestion; only last night because silly Daddy had played with her too long she had been sick all over the lovely carpet in the lounge. Nicola did her best. She said it was nice to be home and entertained Patricia with long stories about choked jets and split ball bearings. She spent Christmas afternoon in the garage taking down the carburettor and on Boxing Day she tightened the brakes, altered the timing, cleaned the plugs and took the car out for a trial run. She went back to London the same night because there was a huge and important ducal order to be coped with next day.

✳ ✳ ✳

Patricia had been stern with herself over Christmas, hadn't allowed herself to remember other Christmases, had fixed her thoughts on next Christmas when surely Elizabeth Rose would be able to travel forty miles without disaster, and Giles would have come to his senses, and another year's social experience would have taught Nicola the entertainment value of long stories about cars. But when Nicola had gone and Patricia had taken down the rather half-hearted decorations, her strung-up spirits sagged and with good sense she suggested to Hugh that they should take a holiday. Hugh disliked going away; he felt uneasy more than ten miles from the Bodleian; hotel food upset his stomach; so he pointed out that Gwen's confinement had cost him sixty guineas; that, since discovering that August's salary was two pounds a week plus, of course, a generous commission, he had been making him an allowance at the rate of three hundred a year; that Nicola had taken him aside and explained how money didn't go nearly as far as you'd expect in London and it was awkward owing Jane ten pounds and not being able to do what other people were doing; and that at any minute Giles might apply for money for his passage home. So Patricia agreed that it would be rash to waste money on a holiday and tried to cheer herself with small gaieties, but it was out of term, there was only a pantomime at the theatre and if she invited people to tea they asked her if August's baby had been born with toenails. She made the depressing discovery that she had no friends. For ten years she had entertained and been entertained by those women whose families were the same age as hers; it hadn't mattered that they'd not been particularly sympathetic because the subject of the children with all its connotations had provided an inexhaustible supply of chat. Better face it, she thought, and she remembered that other time, that wet evening when she had walked up pale Beaumont Street and thought that except for growing older, feebler, uglier, life was over, and then had gone back, rattling in the bus down Botley Road, walking across the meadows, pulling herself in the ferry boat across the dark water, and found them, August and Giles and Nicola, her princes in the land. She had been comforted then, thinking what did it matter if you'd got children, but first August, then Giles, then Nicola had gone, further than any ship or train or aeroplane could have taken them, far over ranges you couldn't climb, seas you couldn't sail, across the intangible deserts of experiences she'd no part in, to lives and loves and hopes in which she had no share. And they'd not gone as princes. The kingdoms she had won for them they had rejected. August with his shiny black bag and his bowler hat, his two pounds a week and his gimcrack villa; Giles dispensing God as a remedy for discontent, boredom or sex repression; Nicola without an idea in her head beyond combustion engines – these weren't the children for whom she'd given up fun and friendship, worked, suffered, worried, taken thought, taken care, done without, suppressed, surrendered and seen her young self die. For the girl she'd been was dead. Anyone less like Patricia Crispin than Mrs Lindsay she couldn't imagine. Lord Waveney's young grand-daughter had had her faults – she'd been tactless, rebellious, hot-tempered, but she'd had her virtues; she'd been fearless, generous and gay.

* * *

Mrs Lindsay had none of those faults and none of those virtues. She was quite a different person. She was patient, amenable, obliging, an economical housekeeper, a sympathetic listener, a peace maker in the home. On most days she drove carefully into Oxford, thinking that in the end a joint, first cold, then hot, then as shepherd's pie, would work out as cheap as Irish stew and cod steaks and cutlets, wondering if by industrious patching the loose covers in the library could be made to last another year. When she didn't drive carefully into Oxford she remained at home, mending, making, ordering her household; and sometimes she went to tea with other such dim disciplined creatures and talked about education and ailments, and sometimes she went out to dinner and people said, 'Here's Mrs Lindsay,' and meant a quiet, pleasant, domesticated gentlewoman in mended black lace or crushed blue velvet, who'd say 'How's Timothy?' and you'd tell her and then say, 'And how are August and Giles?'

How had it come about, this metamorphosis? Well, love's a horse thief. With oats and apples he'd lured the young wild creature. Saying it'll be oats and apples every day for you, he'd slipped on the halter, the collar, harnessed her, and then there'd been no more oats and apples but the long uphill road and the load behind. Because she had spirit and honesty she had pulled to the top of the hill and then love had laughed and said, 'You're worn out,' and taken off the harness and turned her away into the waste that was there instead of the green pastures and the waters of comfort. And now if her Master should come looking for her, how could he recognise her? 'Oh, God,' said Patricia to Hugh, 'what life can do to you!'

* * *

But Hugh didn't understand. He'd found life difficult but that was when he'd been young, before he'd learned that in the face of eternity our lives, that we think so important, are just the sailing of thistledown, the chance-devised hatching and humming of one insect the more. Why hadn't she learned that? He'd been a fighter once; he'd pushed and elbowed and shouted Me, Me; but now he saw the pattern – you got your little fame and it was nothing; you raised your fine children and they were a disappointment to you; your body wore out and you were shovelled underground, and another man stepped forward to profess eighteenth-century literature, and still the sun rose and the thistledown floated, and so it would go on until the ephemeral planet itself grew cold. Why did Patricia go on fighting? She reminded him of a bone-headed colonel sticking to his Salient long after the rest of the army had retired.

He didn't expound his philosophy to Patricia. He knew she hated it, hadn't, he thought, the courage that, curiously enough, is necessary to face the nothingness from which we came. He told her that, after all, most parents were disappointed in their children, that Nicola would marry, that August might make good, that she'd only to wait for someone to invent a new card game and Giles would be applying for his passage home. He said that August was only forty miles away; why didn't she run over and see if there was anything she could do for him? Patricia said, 'There isn't. Gwen attends to his temporal needs *ad nauseam*, and as for anything else "there is a mountain and a wood between us".'

* * *

Hugh said, 'What about running Boy Scouts or something?' so, after that, Patricia took pains to wear a bright face and talk gaily in his presence. She had the house spring-cleaned, arranged flowers in a new way, cut out recipes and went to the theatre. For what was the use of breaking your heart over what couldn't be helped – it's only fools who get themselves hanged for lost causes. She had always had a lot of common sense, had Mrs Lindsay. . . .

CHAPTER FIFTEEN

Pat

I

Hugh was in Oxford. There were tulips in the dining-room, wallflowers in the library and daffodils in the hall. Mrs Frisker had consented to try a new savoury for dinner. Patricia jammed on her new hat, which was mud-coloured and would go with anything, called the puppy and set out for a walk.

The puppy, a seven months old spaniel, had been given to her. She had wanted another wolfhound, a third Shaun, but it had seemed extravagant to spend fifteen guineas on a dog when goodness knew how August was managing or for how long American business men would suffer Giles. Spaniels were cheap to feed, easy to train, so she had accepted Gilbert and sent August a ten-pound note in an Easter egg, and August had written and thanked her very gratefully, saying that he had been able to pay some bills that had been worrying Gwen.

Gilbert was a lovable puppy, but he wasn't a wolfhound. He fawned on tramps but bit tradesmen and the maids. He took no interest in rats but killed chickens. When he stole food, he stole it on early closing day. Already he had wedged his head in the waste pipe of the lavatory basin, fallen out of Patricia's window and been tossed by a bull.

Patricia walked down the lane and at the cross-roads she met Celia Cameron, dressed like herself in brownish tweeds and a mud-coloured hat that would go with anything. She too had a black cocker spaniel. She waited for Patricia and they talked for a few moments about their dogs, gardens and maids. Then Mrs Cameron, who had had her walk, went on down the highroad, and Mrs Lindsay climbed over the stile and took a path through the fields.

It was a lovely day. The sun was shining. Larks were singing. White schooners of clouds were sailing. The wind blew Patricia's hair about. The buttercups were incredibly golden, the grass unbelievably green. Mrs Lindsay saw the buttercups and thought, buttercups. She walked on the grass and didn't think of it. She thought how tiresome Mrs Frisker was about trying new dishes, and wondered how much they would save in coal and what Mrs Frisker would say if she insisted on installing an Aga cooking stove.

Patricia's path led across several fields, through a wood, up a grassy high-banked lane. The lane went over a hill and on past a couple of ugly red brick cottages to a three-mile-distant farm. When Patricia, still thinking about Mrs Frisker, came to the top of the hill, she saw smoke blowing away eastwards on the wind. A bonfire, she thought, or hedge trimmings, but it was the wrong time of year, so she thought, someone's burning rubbish and then, if Mrs Frisker gives notice Agnes will get unsettled too. . . .

✳ ✳ ✳

The lane turned and the smoke blew towards her. Her eyes smarted. They must be burning all the rubbish in the world. And Agnes is tiresome, she thought; they're both tiresome, but they might be so much worse or we might be landed without anyone at all. But it does seem wasteful to spend so much on coal. . . . The lane had curved again. It wasn't rubbish that was burning. It was the cottages.

Patricia called Gilbert and slipped on his lead. Then she ran down past the thorn hedge and the long thin gardens with their beehives, sheds and spring cabbages. Smoke, starred with sparks, was billowing gaily into the treetops. Flames, pale in the sunshine, were licking round the chimney stack. There was a smell of charred wood, the roar of fire and a babel of voices.

'Don't risk it, Tom.'

'Roof 'll be in – that's the next thing.'

'Wait for the fire brigade.'

'Elsie! Elsie!'

The cottages stood sideways to the lane. There was a green gate standing open and a cinder path led to the doors. The front gardens were littered with furniture – windsor chairs, deal tables, a wireless, a mangle, saucepans, toys and pictures. Patricia noticed the Prince Consort lying among the rhubarb leaves.

There were nine people in the garden: an old woman, who had her apron over her head, and an old man who leaned on a stick; a boy of about fifteen, whose face was streaked with sweat and smoke, the woman who was calling 'Elsie', four small chicken and a baby in a high chair. Gilbert was shrinking away from the smoke and noise, so Patricia hooked the lead over the gatepost and then walked up the path.

'What's happened?'

The boy said, 'The cottages are afire.'

'So I see,' said Patricia.

'Our Ted, 'e's gone down to the farm on 'is bike, and there's a chap there with a motorbike as'll go down into Eynsham and telephone for the Brigade.'

The woman who had called for Elsie began to moan. Patricia said, 'What's the matter with her?'

'One of the little 'uns is missing,' said the boy. 'Our mother thought she was playing in the shed but she ain't, so our mother thinks she must 'ave gone up to the back bedroom after 'er doll.'

'But good lord,' said Patricia, 'haven't you done anything?'

'Tom's been in,' said the old man, 'but the smoke beat 'em back. And the staircase 'as gone.'

'Ladder?' snapped Patricia.

'We've got 'im up against the window of the back room. But 'e's too short. Many a time I've said . . .'

'Get it, quick,' said Patricia to the boy. 'We'll put it up where the staircase was. Come on – don't stand there . . .'

They ran round to the back of the house. There was a light ladder, too short to reach the upper windows, standing against the wall. Patricia pulled it down and the boy took one end and she the other. Sparks showered down on them as they hurried back to the door.

'You won't do nothink with that,' said the old man. 'Smoke's too bad. There was a farm'ouse over by Witney . . .'

Tom blundered through the rhubarb, smashing the Prince Consort, bringing the foot of the ladder round. He'd sense and guts, only needed an order, thought Patricia; that's what they all needed . . . some boy like August to shout, 'Come on!' But August was selling refrigerators. . . . She took a firmer grip on the ladder and went through the door.

The room was full of smoke. Her eyes were watering; she couldn't see a thing. But Tom at the end of the ladder was pushing her on and now she saw the stairs. Flames were licking up them. The lower steps were gone.

Between them Patricia and Tom raised the ladder and set it up over the stairs. Then the boy ran out choking. Patricia followed him.

'Told you it was no good, didn't I?' said the old man. 'There was a farm'ouse over by Witney . . .'

Out in the unbelievable sunshine Patricia wiped her eyes on her sleeve and took a deep breath of air. She stripped off her coat, remembered a water butt at the back of the house but hadn't time for that: the ladder would burn. She put her coat over her head, and went back into the smoke-filled room.

She knew where the stair was now, and three strides took her to it. She went up the ladder, her hands scarcely touching the scorching rungs. Thank goodness I'm young and can run up ladders like a monkey, she thought, and looking down from under her coat, saw flames on the passage floor.

But the ladder was resting against something, some beam or, please God, an iron girder that still held. She pulled herself up, remembered they'd said the back bedroom, and groped along the wall. The coat wasn't much good now; she was coughing and choking but here was the door. She reeled into the room; made for the window. It was a casement window and, as she might have known, it wouldn't open. She clenched her fist and smashed it through a pane.

Air when you were choking was better than food when you were hungry or water when you were thirsty or warmth when you were cold, but she only took one breath . . . the ladder would burn. The draught from the broken pane blew the smoke back and she could see a little . . . there was the bed and a small figure bundled down beside it clutching a doll. She lifted the child. It was either dead or unconscious and hung limply over her arm.

Aware of triumph not heat or smoke or lungs that felt like bursting, she reached the door. There was a crash as she passed through it and a shower of sparks. The floor of the passage had fallen and with it the ladder. Gosh, thought Patricia, I'm in a jam. But she wasn't afraid. She was only conscious that for the first time in years life was glorious, that this was life, that here was self, not quiet kind Mrs Lindsay or Mummy or Patricia darling but Pat Crispin, drunk with action, alone, irresponsible and free. God, how life muffled you, the dull dark thing! She shifted the child, placing her arms round it, and jumped into the cloud of smoke below.

The ground was extremely hard. Damn Black August putting her down in a frost . . . one thing was she wouldn't miss much – with the ground like this there'd be no more hunting for a while. Still, it was no use lying there looking like an idiot . . . better get up and crawl if she couldn't run.

✷ ✷ ✷

She tried to rise. But there was something that she mustn't leave . . . no, it was gone and someone had hold of her too, was lifting her. Oh well, someone else was running the show now; she needn't bother. Thankfully she slipped down into silence and the dark. . . .

II

Gwen liked a picture paper. *The Daily Post* gave you four pages of pictures, reported tersely the fall of governments, wars and international crises, but dealt fully with murders, libel cases, breaches of promise, abortion, rape and drapery sales. In spite of what August said about it, Gwen stuck to *The Daily Post*. It wasn't dry.

On the morning of May the fifteenth *The Daily Post* published a photograph of Patricia with August in a smock on her knee. *Oxford Professor's Wife Saves Child from Flames*, said *The Daily Post* and added, *See page four*.

Gwen, who obeyed *The Daily Post* in all things, saw page four. The paragraph was headed, *Scholar's Wife to the Rescue. Child snatched from Death*, and Gwen read on: *While exercising her dog through the peaceful country lanes, willowy, Titian-haired, forty-six-year-old Mrs Patricia Lindsay was horror-stricken to observe a column of flame mounting from the cottage home of Mr Edward Goodenough, stalwart, popular cowman and darts player. Mr Goodenough was absent at market and, on learning from the distracted mother that fair-haired toddler Elsie was not to be located, Mrs Lindsay, despite the protests of neighbours, entered the blazing cottage, groped her way to an upper storey bedroom and carried out the*

192

✱ ✱ ✱

unconscious child only to discover herself trapped by the collapse of the staircase. Leaping from the door of the bedroom into the inferno below and stunned by the fall, Mrs Lindsay was only herself rescued by the prompt arrival of the City Fire Brigade. She was taken by ambulance to the Oxford Infirmary, where she lies suffering from multiple burns and abrasions. When interviewed at his tastefully converted farmhouse at Ferry Hinksey, Professor Lindsay remarked somewhat cryptically, 'It is not the first time that people have been rescued from fires.' In the children's ward of the same hospital, still nursing the favourite doll for which she re-entered the blazing cottage, lies fair-haired Elsie, who recovered consciousness after half an hour of artificial respiration, ably rendered by PC Huggins of the Oxford Constabulary.

Gwen in a mauve wrapper had come down to make the early morning tea. She gave her little squeal of excitement and ran back upstairs.

'David, look! Your mother's in the paper. I'll read it to you.'

August was lying in bed thinking, another bloody morning . . . that bloody Tube . . . the bloody office . . . Henshaw saying, 'You were below your quota last month, Lindsay, and it was April and you've a splendid territory. Now for God's sake pull up your socks and see what you can do. We don't carry passengers . . .' Well, what had Patricia been doing . . . writing an article or something? Probably Gwen was mistaken. An egotist, dying for sensation, she always panicked over *Salesman Commits Suicide* or *Oxford Tradesman's Fall*.

'Let's see,' said August

'I'll read you the bit,' said Gwen.

She constantly read you bits. It never occurred to her that having bits read to you made you want to hit her over the head or scream. August sat up in bed and snatched the paper. Gwen said, 'Oh, David, you *are* rude!'

While August read the paragraph, Gwen thought about Patricia. She didn't like her . . . well, you couldn't respect a person who had dust on her mantelpiece and no tea knives, even if she *was* your mother-in-law. After all, home was a woman's job, wasn't it? Home and children. And there were little things about David which showed that Patricia had neglected him, too. In some ways his manners were good: he raised his hat on all appropriate occasions, stepped off the pavement for ladies, gave up his seat in the Tube; but in other ways they were dreadful: he said 'bloody' like a workman, ate asparagus in his fingers and never said 'Excuse me' after yawning or 'Pardon' if onions or anything repeated. . . . It was all Patricia's fault, of course. Because she couldn't be bothered with the sacred duties of motherhood, she had pushed her children off to rough boarding schools, and in the holidays she had left them to servants while she went dashing off in her car. . . .

August said, 'Lor'.'

Gwen said, 'Fancy her doing that at her age. Good of her, wasn't it? but I should have thought she would have considered her husband before a workman's child.'

'What *do* you mean?' said August and in parenthesis, 'Coo lumme, look at me!'

'Oh, David, don't use that common expression. Think of Baby. What I mean is, supposing she'd been burned to death, what would your father have done?'

'At moments like that,' said August, 'you don't think of your father, I mean your husband, at all.'

'Oh, David, d'you mean that if you were in the same position you wouldn't think of me?'

'No,' said August, 'I mean yes. What I mean is, I shouldn't think of you.'

'Nor of Baby?'

'Good God, no.'

'Well, I think that's dreadful,' said Gwen, getting off the bed and gathering up *The Daily Post*. 'Why, even in the war they took the single men first. Hark, there's the kettle!' She left the room.

August lay down. He thought how odd it was to hear someone really say, 'Hark!' and he hoped to God that there would soon be another war. He'd enlist at once – that would be much the quickest way of getting to the front. On the morning that war was declared he'd put on his bowler hat and take his little black bag and start off towards the station as smug as usual but he'd never arrive at the bloody office; he'd blow into the nearest recruiting place and he wouldn't tell Gwen until afterwards. But there wouldn't be a war . . . that blasted Anthony Eden would see to it . . . and how ever many cottages got set on fire, he wouldn't be there . . . Mummy had all the luck . . . Mummy. . . .

He began to think about Patricia. It was extraordinary what a nebulous character she seemed. As a small boy he had been awfully fond of her, but that had probably been a complex of some kind, because, later on, she had become just one of the people who mustn't find out . . . though only God knew why there'd been such a lot to find out . . . it hadn't all been things like Gwen and the sherry party; there'd been a perfect host of things that he couldn't imagine making secrets of now – things like being friends with a boy called Cuthbert, and trying to write poetry, and liking Greta Garbo. Well, there Patricia had been . . . a parent . . . someone who might find out; and he hadn't ever wondered what sort of a woman she was; whether she too had friends with silly names, tried to write poetry, invented idiotic stories about saving lives and dying gloriously. Perhaps she didn't, but he didn't know that either; he couldn't say that it was like her to go into a burning cottage and fetch a kid out, and he couldn't say whatever had come over her? He simply didn't know what she was like. It was a pity. If she hadn't been his mother he might, he thought, have liked her. As it was, his feeling for her was that she was part of home and the good old days before he'd made a fool of himself – that, and a quite sincere and lively gratitude for remembered kindnesses. But you didn't love people because they'd been kind and you were grateful. Not counting falling in love, which, of course, was a temporary insanity designed by nature with the sole object of causing you to reproduce your species, you loved people because you liked them. . . .

'Here you are, David. Here's your nice cup of tea. Sit up and drink it before it gets cold, dear.'

'Gwen,' said August, 'why do you like me?'

Gwen dimpled. Here they were, been married over a year, and David still said this kind of thing to her. Of course she could take some credit for it. She wasn't like some girls. In spite of all the cooking and housework, she'd kept her hands

* * *

nice; when Baby was coming she had taken the special care of her hair and complexion, which that helpful Flora Dyson in *The Daily Post* advised. And she never allowed herself to get nervy and snap at David; if she felt in the least bit run down she instantly went out for a good-sized bottle of that marvellous Nixon's Nightcap. And she'd always remembered a very frank but so nicely-put article by Flora Dyson about mystery and what it means to men . . . she'd never let David catch her looking unattractive. . . . So here they were.

She sat down on August's bed.

'You silly boy! I ought to be getting on but never mind, I'll make up for it afterwards. Funny, isn't it, how I've always got time for you? Well, David dear, I like you because you're so big and protective – that's one thing. And because you work so hard for me and Baby and come home to us every night instead of staying in London and going to horrid clubs and things. And I like you because you're such a loyal hubby – Baby and I know that you'd stick to us through thick and thin. And then I like you – of course I know I ought to say that I'd like you just as much if you were getting thin on top and wore glasses, but I do like you just a teeny bit more because I've got eyes in my head and I know quite well that other girls look at you and wish they were me.'

August had emptied his cup. He put it down on the bed-side table that was still his by the grace of the nebulous person, who had suddenly and unaccountably sent him a ten-pound note in a Mickey Mouse Easter Egg. She's a wraith, he thought; perhaps if I read *The Daily Post* with more attention I might give her a sort of substance, the same sort of substance that Gwen has given me. But it wouldn't be her any more than Gwen's loyal hardworking husband, whom other girls look at, is me. Oh well, thought August, saying, 'I *must* get up,' swinging out his legs and sitting on the edge of his bed, another bloody morning . . . the bloody Tube. . . .

III

Peter said, 'You know your mother must be rather a fine person. It's odd that you didn't manage to change her.'

Giles considered Patricia. 'I think it's much more difficult with one's own people,' he got out. 'You see, Peter, one is so near to them that they're out of focus, blurred; one doesn't really know what they're like, so one can't find the angle.'

'I see what you mean,' said Peter, putting down the news-paper and lying back against the red and white waterproof cushions lavishly piled on his long chair. He and Giles were digesting in the sun porch of the Newbiggin home on Cape Cod. Soon they'd be going to bathe.

'But,' said Peter, 'I do feel that one ought to be able to find the angle. You're not living with her now. It's your chance to step back and take a good look at her.'

Obediently Giles tried. He closed his eyes. There was Patricia coming into the schoolroom. Her hair was untidy. She had straw in it. Her hands had garden mould on them. She said, 'Hullo, Giles, stuffing indoors as usual. . . .'

He said, 'She's an out-of-doors sort of person. But not definitely hearty. She hasn't got much taste – I don't mean that we have antimacassars but she's apt to buy dogs cut out of wood and have photographs. She does all sorts of jobs in the garden but I don't know if it's because she likes doing them or because they've got to be done. She isn't fashionable but I don't know whether she'd like to be or whether she can't afford it. She likes animals. She wanted my brother to go into the Army.'

Peter said, 'Well, I should call her hearty.'

'No, she isn't really. She doesn't do anything athletic.'

'What are her difficulties?'

'As far as I know she hasn't any. One of those impossible people who take life as they find it.'

Peter said, 'Contented? Then the angle is: what has God done for her? And this affair in the paper – it does give you a handle. I mean she must realise Who sent her in the direction of those cottages.'

'I daresay she does. She goes to church, you know, but, as I told her quite frankly, she keeps God with her Sunday hat in the wardrobe.'

'How did she react?'

'She said things like shut up and don't be idiotic.'

Peter frowned.

'So you see how difficult it is,' said Giles plaintively.

As he spoke Mrs Newbiggin came through the door leading from the playroom. Here was no characterless Patricia, but a woman you could sum up at sight and find your angle. She was rich, handsome, childless, had moved for years in fast-stepping American society and discovered its emptiness. Bored to death, she had yearned for some new thing, and Peter and Giles had supplied the novelty. Her husband, a mild little man with his heart in his second establishment, was grateful to them. He hoped they would make a long long stay at Parklands.

Sonia Newbiggin said, 'Dear Peter . . . dear Giles, the Hispano-Suiza is at the door if you feel like bathing. . . .'

CHAPTER SIXTEEN

Return

I

The green casement curtains were drawn but the sun had found the chinks and streamed in, making odd geometrical patterns on the walls of the private ward, designed to meet the needs of the middle classes. Patricia was supposed to be resting, but her hands didn't hurt her now, nor her back, provided she lay still, and she had slept all night. She lay with her eyes open looking at Nicola's lilac.

August had written, hoping she was all right; business was OK and Elizabeth Rose was taking notice; the kitchen ceiling had fallen into the beefsteak pie and they had had to have the builders in, which was a nuisance.

Hugh had been in and out. His porridge had been lumpy, the bath water tepid; oughtn't the marmalade pot to be washed daily?

Nicola had sent lilac. *It's rather like sending coals to Newcastle but I thought you would like it better than orchids*, she had remarked.

* * *

Patricia looked at the lilac and wondered why Nicola had thought she would like it better than orchids and the answer came, because I'm Mummy and of course mothers like simple fragrant flowers like lilac and not luxurious exotic hothouse things. Patricia smiled. How little they knew of her, sending her news of kitchen ceilings, telling her about lumpy porridge and sticky jam jars, sending her lilac instead of orchids! *Oh, to love, to be so loved and so mistaken* . . . thought Patricia, for she knew now who and what she was, could, if she'd had the art, have gone on, summed up, declared herself, broken the extraordinary barrier of familiarity, relationship, duty and pre-conception that lies between the generations, between us all.

But she hadn't the art and anyhow, they wouldn't have believed her. Mummy, Mummy they'd called and she'd answered, 'Yes, dear,' and God knew whom they had called to – Himself, perhaps – but they hadn't called to Pat Crispin. Someone had answered: they'd seen and felt her and there she'd been, kind quiet Mrs Lindsay. And Mrs Lindsay had walked the earth, a wraith, contented because that was right but never gloriously happy; she had been liked because we all like kind quiet people, loved because you always love your mother, and all the time, while the wraith walked, Pat Crispin, who was real and substantial, had slept, never batting an eyelid, in that deep grave we dig to bury our souls. She had slept soundly and long but not too late. Oh, it hadn't been much of a show, just going in there and fetching out a kid who, she'd since learned, was mentally deficient, illegitimate and would have been better dead, but somehow or another it

* * *

had served to wake Pat Crispin and Patricia knew now what she was, what she'd be when the time came to put off life's stuffy garment and step out into the unknown, alone and irresponsible and gloriously free. . . .

There was no one she could tell about it. Hugh thought that when you died that was that – nothing; poor fool, for his information he relied on a lot of disgusting-looking grey matter that a biff or a tumour could make lunatic; he relied on a mortal thing for information about immortality; he'd never known a moment when you were near to death – the garment slipping – and you knew. And she couldn't tell Giles. He believed you'd a soul but not what you might call a self-soul: he believed that you listened, were guided, could share, not stand, fight, fall alone. August very probably believed in the resurrection of the body and a heaven where you bathed all day except when you were riding to hounds. And Nicola she suspected of sharing Hugh's dismal theory. But it didn't matter. You were lonely, but you had to be lonely to keep your soul.

Well, where was she? She was forty-six with scarcely a tooth left in her lower jaw; she was disappointed in her children; her husband no longer took any sexual interest in her; her hair was fading; she'd done most things. But what did it matter? Life was a parenthesis, a muddled phrase too often annotated. Why worry over it? Read on, read on. . . .

'Well, Mrs Lindsay,' said Nurse, entering briskly. 'Have you had a nice sleep?'

'Yes, thank you, Nurse,' said Patricia.

'That's right.' She crossed the room and drew back the green curtains. 'I expect you'd like a wash and brush up,

***

wouldn't you? Professor Lindsay's coming to tea with you today.'

Patricia's hands were still bandaged. Nurse washed her face, powdered her nose and combed her hair.

She said, 'Lovely your hair must have been when you were a girl.'

Patricia was barely what Nurse called 'straight' when Hugh came in. Always ill at ease in a sick room, he stood about saying, 'Well, well. Well, well.'

Patricia looked at him with new eyes. It wasn't only that his hair had gone grey and his skin leathery. He wasn't the same person. He wasn't the man she had married. You couldn't imagine this Hugh kneeling on the floor of a railway carriage reading George Herbert: you couldn't imagine that Hugh standing about your sick room with nothing to say but, 'Well, well.'

'Well, well,' she said before she could stop herself, and then, 'Sit down, Hugh.'

Hugh sat down and asked how she was feeling and Patricia said she was feeling perfectly all right but tired of dabs and caramel pudding and ravenous for beef steak and onions or chops – bloody ones.

Hugh smiled. '*The Mark of the Beast* – he knew his stuff, such as it was,' he said.

A wardmaid carried in a tray of tea. Hugh poured out.

Patricia said, 'I've heard from August. And Nicola sent those flowers.'

'Did August say how he was getting on? In that business of his, I mean.'

✱ ✱ ✱

'He said business was OK.'

'He always does unless he says it's splendid. I don't see how they can manage on four hundred a year.'

'We managed in Glasgow.'

'We had more than that,' said Hugh.

'Yes, but the cost of living was higher; it was fantastic. And August has a much better housekeeper than you had, my dear.'

'Nonsense,' said Hugh kindly. 'Once you'd adapted yourself, you got on very well.'

Patricia gave a snort of indignation. Hugh looked up from his rock bun surprised.

'I didn't adapt myself,' said Patricia. 'I was caught by life and shut up in a cage. So I got tame.'

'Well,' said Hugh, 'you can put it like that, but we've all got to learn to fit in.'

'Not learn,' she objected. 'Forget.'

'This is a very odd conversation,' said Hugh.

Patricia said, 'We used to talk about that kind of thing.'

Hugh said, 'We've grown up since then.'

'We've grown into very funny shapes,' said Patricia. 'Like plants, you know, that have had boxes or something put on top of them. Don't you think so?'

'No,' said Hugh. 'What I think is that you've been lying here letting your imagination run away with you. Haven't you got anything to read?'

'Heaps, but it makes my back ache.'

'Of course you can't knit.'

'Hugh,' said Patricia, 'I'm never going to knit again. I hate knitting.'

'I thought you liked it.'

'I know you did. Nicola thought I liked lilac better than orchids. Celia Cameron came yesterday and she brought me *Good Housekeeping* and *Woman and Home*. But I don't want to read them. What I want to read is a paper called *Horse and Hound*. I want to look at the advertisements. I'm going,' said Patricia rather nervously because you can preach and nobody minds, but practise and the fat's in the fire, 'to buy a horse of my own.'

'You can't start riding again,' said Hugh, 'at your age. You'll only break your neck.'

'There are worse things than breaking one's neck,' said Patricia.

Then Hugh's mind went back. Dimly he saw the façade of Hulver, the marble steps, the urns, the fountains, and there was a clatter of hoofs and Patricia, 'a young thing not know-ing then what the world was', mounted on a tall black horse that had won the Grand National, made that sudden dramatic entrance. . . . So she was trying to go back. *On revient toujours à ses premiers amours* . . . A Frenchman, of course; they could always say it; they could say it enchantingly but measure them beside Milton, Wordsworth and you knew that you were drinking champagne. You couldn't go back in life; you'd learned; you'd grown. But giving advice was no good, especially giving advice to women . . . she'd better buy her horse and she'd soon discover that she'd grown out of all that. . . .

'Well,' he said, 'do as you please about it but don't blame me if you're soon back here – that's all.'

✱ ✱ ✱

II

Hugh was in Oxford. Giles was in Sweden. Nicola was in London and would be coming home for the weekend bringing Michael, who was a racing motorist and a sweet thing. August had written to ask if Hugh or Patricia would be awfully kind and guarantee a small overdraft.

They hadn't called 'Mummy!' in vain. Patricia was going to guarantee August's overdraft. She was going to be charming to Michael and ask him questions about engines. But in the meantime, sitting astride the roan mare that some previous owner had optimistically named Swift, with the cold November rain dripping off her hat and soaking through the knees of her breeches, with her heart in her mouth and no care in the world, she listened for the sound of a hound speaking.

It came, and 'Huic to Ravager', and the whole pack crashing into music. Out from the larch copse they streamed, flashes of white, black and tan across the brown furrows. Swift turned on her hocks and was away round the headland. The rain beat in Patricia's face and she heard the wind singing.

III

Gwen said, 'Fancy your mother riding about chasing foxes.'

August said, 'Oh well, I expect she only potters.'

'Still,' said Gwen, 'I should have thought that at her age she would have been glad to sit down by a nice fire and knit some little things for Baby. . . .'

* * *

IV

Nicola said, 'Well, my sweet, what did you think of them?'

'Your father,' said Michael, treading on the accelerator, 'terrifies me. I mean he's a Professor and all that, isn't he? I was terrified of your mother at first, too – thought I'd have to talk about huntin'. But it was all right. We talked cars. She's quite a dear, isn't she?'

V

Thelma, who was thinking of being changed and going to England with Giles and Peter, said, 'Wot is your moder like, Giles, tell me?'

'Well, she's tall,' said Giles, 'and her hair's red . . .' and he stuck there.